LEARNING TO LOVE

NATALIE ANN

AUTHOR'S NOTE

ALSO BY NATALIE ANN

Trevor Miles and Riley Hamilton – Last Chance

Matt Winters and Dena Hall- Another Chance

Logan Taylor and Kennedy Miles- It's My Chance

Justin Cambridge and Taryn Miles – One More Chance

The Fierce Five Series

Gavin Fierce and Jolene O'Malley- How Gavin Stole Christmas

Brody Fierce and Aimee Reed - Brody

Aiden Fierce and Nic Moretti- Aiden

Mason Fierce and Jessica Corning- Mason

Cade Fierce and Alex Marshall - Cade

Ella Fierce and Travis McKinley- Ella

Fierce Family

Sam Fierce and Dani Rhodes- Sam

Bryce Fierce and Payton Davies - Bryce

Drake Fierce and Kara Winslow – Drake

Noah Fierce and Paige Parker - Noah

Wyatt Fierce and Adriana Lopez – Wyatt

Jade Fierce and Brock James – Jade

Ryder Fierce and Marissa McMillan – Ryder

Fierce Matchmaking

Devin Andrews and Hope Hall- Devin

Mick McNamara and Lindsey White- Mick

Cody McMillian and Raina Davenport – Cody

Liam O'Malley and Margo West- Liam

Walker Olson and Stella White – Walker

Flynn Slater and Julia McNamara – Flynn

Ivan Andrews & Kendra Key- Ivan

Jonah Davenport & Megan Harrington- Jonah

Royce Kennedy & Chloe Grey- Royce

Sawyer Brennan & Faith O'Malley- Sawyer

Trent Davenport & Roni Hollister- Trent

Gabe McCarthy & Elise Kennedy – Gabe

Ben Kelley & Eve Hall – Ben

Paradise Place

Josh Turner and Ruby Gentile – Cupid's Quest

Harris Walker and Kaelyn Butler – Change Up

Philip Aire and Blair McKay- Starting Over

Nathan Randal and Brina Shepard – Eternal

Ryan Butler and Shannon Wilder – Falling Into Love

Brian Dawson and Robin Masters – Mistletoe Magic

Caden Finley and Sarah Walker- Believe In Me

Evan Butler and Parker Reed – Unexpected Delivery

Trey Bridges and Whitney Butler – Forever Mine

Dylan Randal and Zoe Milton- Because Of You

Cash Fielding and Hannah Shepard – Letting Go

Brent Elliot and Vivian Getman – No More Hiding

Marcus Reid and Addison Fielding- Made For Me

Rick Masters and Gillian Bridges – The One

Cooper Winslow and Morgan Finely- Back To Me

Jeremy Reid and McKenna Preston- Saving Me

Christian Butler and Liz Carter- Begin Again

Cal Perkins and Mia Finley- Angels Above

Amore Island

Family Bonds- Hunter and Kayla

Family Bonds- Drew and Amanda

Family Bonds – Mac and Sidney

Family Bonds- Emily & Crew

Family Bonds- Ava & Seth

Family Bonds- Eli & Bella

Family Bonds- Hailey & Rex

Family Bonds- Penelope & Griffin

Family Bonds- Bode & Samantha

Family Bonds- Hudson & Delaney

Family Bonds- Alex & Jennie

Family Bonds- Roark & Chelsea

Family Bonds- Duke & Hadley

Family Bonds – Carter & Avery

Family Bonds- Egan & Blake

Family Bonds- Carson & Laine

Family Bonds- Grace & Lincoln

Blossoms

A Love for Lily – Zane Wolfe and Lily Bloom

A Playboy For Poppy- Reese McGill and Poppy Bloom

A Romantic For Rose – Thomas Klein and Rose Bloom

A Return For Ren – Ren Whitney and Zara Wolfe

A Journey For Jasmine- Wesley Wright and Jasmine Greene

A Vacationer for Violet – Violet Soren And Trace Mancini

A Hero For Heather- Heather Davis and Luke Remington

A Doctor For Daisy- Daisy Jones And Theo James

An Investigator For Ivy- Ivy Greene and Brooks Scarsdale

A Date For Dahlia- Dahlia Greene and Hugh Crosby

A Surprise For Sage- Sage Mancini and Knox Bradford

Looking For Love

Learning To Love – West Carlisle and Abby Sherman

Love To The Rescue – Braylon Carlisle and Lilian Baker

Love Collection

Vin Steele and Piper Fielding – Secret Love

Jared Hawk and Shelby McDonald – True Love

Erik McMann and Sheldon Case – Finding Love

Connor Landers and Melissa Mahoney- Beach Love

Ian Price and Cam Mason- Intense Love

Liam Sullivan and Ali Rogers - Autumn Love

Owen Taylor and Jill Duncan - Holiday Love

Chase Martin and Noelle Bennett - Christmas Love

Zeke Collins and Kendall Hendricks - Winter Love

Troy Walker and Meena Dawson – Chasing Love

Jace Stratton and Lauren Towne - First Love

Gabe Richards and Leah Morrison - Forever Love

Blake Wilson and Gemma Anderson – Simply Love

Brendan St. Nicholas and Holly Lane – Gifts of Love

ABOUT THE AUTHOR

Sign up for my newsletter for up to date releases and deals.
Newsletter.

Follow me on:

Website
    Twitter
    Facebook
    Pinterest
    Goodreads
    Bookbub

As always reviews are always appreciated as they help potential readers understand what a book is about and boost rankings for search results.

BLURB

Billionaire West Carlisle has put his career and amassing his fortune first in his life. He's the oldest of eight kids and has been the fill-in dad since he was eighteen. After meeting a blonde-haired beauty, he realizes he's not ready to let her go. But how will she feel when she finds out he's not just a regular guy on vacation?

Abby Sherman has always been a dreamer. She wants the quintessential family with a white picket fence. What she got growing up was a single father and a mother who couldn't be bothered to put her daughters first, second, or maybe even third. A trip of a lifetime lands in her lap where she meets a man that piques her interest to do something she's never imagined she would do. She has no future plans after her week with West and even less once she finds out who he really is. Yet he is determined to give her everything she's ever wanted. She just has to open her heart and throw away her fear of being left again and make him understand it's not money she is after.

PROLOGUE

"Why the sad face, Abby?" Liz asked her. "It's your birthday."

She looked at her older sister of seven years. Liz was thirteen, Abby just turning six. She wished she was older and they could hang out together more. But her sister had friends and got to be with them.

Well, not during the day on summer break. Their father worked long hours with his own fencing company and they had a sitter here.

A sitter to watch her while Liz got to do her own things most times.

Abby shrugged. "Don't know," she said.

"Sure, you do," Liz said, moving in to sit on the bed next to Abby. "Dad will be home any minute with pizza and cake. Aren't you hungry? You got to pick out your dinner like we always do."

Her father was great like that. He did everything for them. He cooked, he cleaned, he gave them special dinners for their birthdays.

He couldn't be their mother though and Lily Sherman

wasn't around. When she was around, she wasn't present. Abby knew that well enough even if she wished it weren't so.

She just couldn't fully understand what was wrong with her mother, and for a young girl craving love and attention from an adult female, she didn't care there was more bad than good with her mother's visits.

"I know," she said.

Liz reached her hand out and rubbed it on Abby's thigh. "Dad is trying to make it a good day for you. He even took the afternoon off and we went to play mini golf like you asked."

Her father worked a lot in the summer. Early mornings and long days. She didn't see him as much as she wanted but understood he had to do what needed to be done.

Nope, she didn't understand that. She just had been told that enough by Liz.

"I beat you too," she said, cracking the barest of grins.

"You did," Liz said. "You're better than me."

She was positive Liz had let her win. Her sister played a lot of sports and was good at them. The last thing she wanted was to be *allowed* to win because it was her birthday.

Or worse yet, because she was the baby of the family and everyone had to protect her.

"I don't think so," Abby said. She still was looking at the coloring book on her lap. She hadn't picked a crayon up to apply it to the pages since Liz came in.

"I know you want Mom to be here," Liz said.

She turned her head to look at her sister. "She said she'd come for my birthday."

Liz sighed. "That was months ago. We haven't talked to her since."

"Why does she come and then go away and not talk

to us?"

"No one knows exactly," Liz said. "Mom is sick. Dad told us that."

"She looks fine when we see her," she argued.

"Sick in another way," Liz said. "You know that. She needs help and until she gets it fully, it's too hard. See how much she upsets you when she comes and then leaves again? Don't you want to have things be normal?"

"What's normal?" she asked, crying. "None of my friends have this problem. Even the ones whose parents don't live together, they still see their mothers."

Liz hugged her. "I know, Abby. But what fun is normal? Why not be different?"

"I don't like being different," she said, sniffling. "I just want Mom to be here for my birthday."

Abby knew there wasn't anything her sister could do about it. She didn't understand why her father couldn't fix it though. He fixed everything else in life that she asked of him.

"If she could be here, I'm sure she would be," Liz said.

"There is still time for her to show up," she said, hoping.

Her sister moved out of her arms and didn't say a word about her statement.

"Why don't we go get the plates out and set the table? Then when Dad gets here we can eat the pizza steaming hot and have the roof of our mouths burned with the cheese dripping everywhere."

Abby smiled. "That's the best way to eat it."

The two of them jumped off her bed and went to the kitchen.

The plates were out and down, the table set and they heard two car doors.

She ran to the front to look out the window, saw it was

only the neighbor and came back.

"Who was it?" Liz asked.

"I thought it was Mom. It was just the Smiths."

Her mother didn't have a car last she knew. If she came, someone would have to bring her.

Or maybe since her father seemed to be gone so long for the food, he was picking their mother up as a surprise.

Yeah, that had to be it!

"You just got a big smile on your face," Liz said. "What's going through your head?"

"Do you think Dad is getting Mom? He's been gone a long time."

Liz sighed. "Don't get your hopes up, Abby. He's not. They are probably just busy at the pizza place. He had to get your cake too."

"But you don't know," she argued. "Dad could be surprising you too."

Liz didn't bother to answer and got the glasses down. "Do you want milk with dinner?"

"Sure," she said.

When her father came in the door ten minutes later, all he had with him was a pizza box and a cake.

She tried to keep the sadness from her face. The tears back too.

"There is the birthday girl ready to eat this whole pizza," her father said.

She giggled. He could always make her laugh.

"I'm going to eat more than you," she said.

"Then we should eat it while it's hot, and you can open your gifts after the cake."

She wondered what she got. She only asked for two things. The new Beach Barbie and the outdoor playset that came with summer clothing.

Liz had never been interested in Barbies and there weren't any to hand down to her. But her mother gave her her first Barbie a few years ago and she treasured it and wanted to continue to add to her collection and play house when she could.

That perfect life she always dreamed and wished for. What she thought a normal family had.

When they were stuffed with pizza, her father brought the cake out with the six candles on it lit.

"Close your eyes," Liz said. "Make a wish and blow them out."

The pink cake was placed in front of her. She knew it was chocolate flavored, her favorite. The candles were pink and white stripes and the flames flickered fast.

She closed her eyes, wished that her mother would show up and then took a deep breath and blew with everything she had.

"They all went out," her father said. "Good girl."

She opened her eyes and still only saw her father and sister there.

Her father handed her a few boxes, she ripped into them and got exactly what she'd asked for from him. Like she always did.

She couldn't wait to go to her room and play.

"I can play house with you if you want," Liz said.

Her sister never offered. "Please," she said, smiling.

It was turning into a great night after all, but when she was in bed by herself and the lights were out, her mother not only didn't show up, she didn't even call to wish her a happy birthday.

Abby felt the tears slipping down her cheeks and realized she should have listened to her sister and not gotten her hopes up.

1

THE BAD GUY

Twenty-One Years Later

"I'm telling you, Talia, your job is to graduate. You better damn well do it," West Carlisle said to his baby sister. She was fourteen years younger than him and the last of the eight kids to finish college. He was getting too old to keep doing this and was thrilled it might finally be over.

"You're not my father," Talia snapped. "Stop treating me like your child."

He lifted his eyebrow at her. He was trying his hardest not to lose his shit over this repetitive argument. He'd thought Rowan who was the sixth kid was the hard one to keep focused and in school, but it was nothing like Talia.

His sister could be testy and emotional and the snapping at him was nothing new.

"Your sister is right," his mother said, walking into the room.

"Mom," he said. "You and I agreed. You even asked me to come here to talk to her."

"Mom!" Talia shouted. "You always do this. You say you're on my side and then you call West in to act like the bad guy."

This time he looked at his mother with his arms crossed. "Are you playing us?" he asked his mother.

His mother smiled. "No. But you two need to talk and you need to do it in person. Talia, grow up. You've got one month left to graduate, then you're done. It's like pulling teeth to get you to go back each semester. I don't understand it. You enjoy school."

"No," Talia said. "You think I enjoy it because I have fun with my friends. But I hate sitting in class. I hate doing the work."

"A career isn't just handed to anyone," West said. "You know that and I know it."

Just because he supported the entire family now and paid for their education didn't mean he handed it over.

Talia had to work during breaks for spending money. Those were the rules. He didn't care if she served fast food, babysat, tended bar, or did social media bullshit like most of the rest of her generation.

All she had to do was earn some damn money.

She did. She made jewelry and accessories and sold them online.

She did well enough that she wanted to quit college multiple times and focus on that.

He'd said no way.

"I make enough to live off of what I'm doing now," Talia said.

"Only because your brother pays for living expenses,"

his mother said. "Your car. Your insurance. You live at home with me when you aren't in school."

The second half of his siblings got more than the first half.

Early on, he was still in college and working multiple jobs, investing what he could and building an empire on sweat, risks and sheer determination.

His siblings closer to him in age incurred college debt, but he cleared it for them once he could.

Every single one of them worked for him or a company he acquired or invested in.

But, as he'd told his sister many times, nothing was free and they were going to earn it.

"I can live on my own," Talia argued.

He snorted. "Go ahead. Try it."

Talia lifted her chin. Just like she'd been doing since she was four.

He'd never forget the day they'd found out his father had died overseas. Sam Carlisle's life ended way too soon at forty years old serving his country.

He'd left a wife and eight kids back at Fort Bragg, North Carolina.

At eighteen and his senior year of high school, it was on West to step up and be the man.

His siblings didn't care for it all that much, but everyone was thanking him now.

Talia might at some point too. Maybe.

"You always make it so hard," Talia said, stomping her foot.

"Newsflash," he almost snarled. "Life is hard."

"Your brother is right," his mother said. "Stop being a spoiled brat."

Talia's jaw dropped. His might have followed. His

mother never said anything like that to Talia. Even if he thought it was true.

He supposed most times the baby of the family got spoiled more than the rest.

"I'm not a brat," Talia argued.

"If it smells like a brat. And looks like a brat. Then I guess maybe it's a brat," his mother said.

West ran his hands through his hair. Good lord, this seemed to be less about Talia and more about his mother and Talia arguing like never before.

"What is going on here?" he asked.

"Mom is being annoying," Talia said. "I'm done with school in a month. I'm not sure what the big deal is. I complain all the time."

"That's right," his mother said. "It's all you ever do. Complain, complain, complain. You've got an easy life. One that I never had. I raised eight children on my own before your father even passed."

"No one said you needed to keep getting pregnant."

"Talia!" he snapped this time. "Uncalled for."

"What?" Talia said. "It's like every time Dad came home for a period of time Mom got pregnant. She knew what life was like with him in the service. You said all the time you moved so much early on. I don't understand why her life choices have to be compared to mine."

His sister had a point. "Mom, what's going on with you? You're never this testy either."

"She's upset that I want to move out," Talia said. "Be honest with West. You got him here, tell him the real reason we are fighting so much."

This was all news to him. Though the truth was, he barely had time to eat and sleep, let alone keep up with all the family drama.

He lived in a penthouse in Manhattan. Had a weekend home in the Hamptons. His brother Braylon worked in the same building as him and they barely saw each other, let alone talked about family.

The rest of his siblings he saw or talked to even less. No one had time and everyone had jobs.

"Mom?" he asked. "Is Talia right?"

"Maybe I'm not ready for her to move out. She wants to when she graduates. She can't afford it."

"I'm going to get roommates," Talia said proudly.

"We all moved out," he argued.

"Talia is the last," his mother said.

He let out a sigh. He didn't have time for this. "I flew all this way to talk to Talia about finishing her last month of college and it's more about the fact that you want her to stay living in the basement when she's home on break?" he asked. "That is what this is about?"

"You're the one in trouble now, Mom," Talia said, smirking. "She made me come home this weekend too because you'd be here."

If there was one thing he hated in life it was being manipulated. Even by those he loved.

"Talia, are you going to finish college?"

"Of course I am," his sister said. "I've hated every minute of the four years of classes, but I wouldn't let it go now that I've come this far."

"Fine," he said. "Then go back to your friends."

Talia crossed her arms. "Excuse me. Are you dismissing me?"

"Yes," he said. "Unless you want to stay and get more of a lecture."

"Nope," Talia said. "I'm out of here."

"I'll see you at graduation," he said to her.

"I'll have you all together again," his mother said.

It seemed to be the only time they all were together. Some major event and he had to be the one to ensure everyone returned for it.

"Now it's your turn," he said to his mother.

Once Talia was out the door, his mother started to laugh. "That was easier than I thought."

He eyed her. She wasn't mad or nasty or anything like she was minutes ago. "What was?"

"Getting you to believe what just happened."

He growled. "You two set this up?" Just like he hated. Manipulation. And his mother was a pro. Better than he'd give her credit for.

"Yep," his mother said. "Talia and I get along just fine. She's not going anywhere just yet and you know it."

He felt like an idiot. There were very few homes in North Carolina that had a basement. Let alone a basement apartment. But he'd had the house built for his mother so that while each one of the kids was in college in the past ten years, they had their own space to come and go. The rest had their own spaces in the house. One over the garage, another a wing to themselves. Everyone had a room. Something he and the oldest four siblings had never experienced living at home.

His family didn't lack for much now and he made sure of it.

"Explain to me why you just did the one thing you know I can't stand."

"Westerly Samuel, don't take that tone with me. I brought you into this world, I can push you out."

He snorted. She'd used those words plenty in his life. To his siblings too.

"You've got an agenda then, so tell me what it is."

"You're burning yourself out. When was the last time you had a vacation?"

He couldn't believe this. "I don't know," he said. "Why does that matter?"

"It matters because in the past six months every single one of your siblings has called me bitching about you."

"Excuse me?" he asked. He was the boss. No one bitched about him behind his back.

"That's right," his mother said. "Everyone is worried or ticked. Maybe both at the same time. I'm over it. You're not everyone's father. You don't need to shoulder this. You never did. Even though I and everyone in the family have appreciated what you've done and sacrificed, you can stop now."

"Stop what?" he asked. "And you haven't said what everyone is bitching about."

"Do you want me to throw them all under the bus?" his mother asked.

"Since I'm the one putting the fuel in the bus, you can keep talking," he said, crossing his arms.

He was an ass saying that, but he wanted to know. It's not like his mother didn't trick him to get here.

"Fine," his mother said. "Braylon says you're at the office before anyone else and leave after everyone else. That lately you've been snapping more than normal and people are coming to him. He's tired of putting fires out and worrying about lawsuits or people leaving."

Braylon was kid number two and an attorney based in Manhattan working at his headquarters. He saw that brother the most and even then it's not like it was weekly.

"This is all news to me," he said.

"Take it up with your brother. Moving on...Laken. She said you're driven to keep buying more and more businesses. Like you're on a mission to diversify enough that her head is spinning and she doesn't even know what city she is in anymore."

His sister was kid number three. She was in charge of making sure all the businesses acquired or invested in followed his policies and procedures. She went in and laid the groundwork. Kind of like a consultant, and her communications degree and smooth way about her made it the perfect position for her.

"Again, she hasn't said a word to me. She can take some time off. I'd never say no."

"She will when she can," his mother said. "But I think she is afraid of letting you down."

He didn't like hearing that. "She couldn't do that."

"Maybe you should sit down and talk to her like an older brother and not her boss. Let her know those things. You know, ask her questions rather than giving her orders." He pulled his phone out and started to type. "I'm talking to you. Put the device away."

"I'm sending an email to Laken to schedule a meeting for us."

"See," his mother said. "That's being her boss, not her brother."

Shit. She was right. He put his phone away.

"I'll call her when I'm back."

"Good. Now there is Foster. He's good at keeping away from you."

Sibling number four. Foster handled all the technology for him and every other business under him. Went in and set it up and made sure they were secure on top of it.

"I haven't seen Foster in months."

"Yeah," his mother said. "Pretty sad when you work together."

"He's hardly ever in the office," he argued. "He hates Manhattan."

His brother was set up offsite and took care of things outside the city. He came in when he needed to but hated the people and the congestion.

"That's right," his mother said. "You know your siblings well enough to make sure they are happy and able to perform at peak levels for you."

That sounded cold and he knew she was trying to make her point. "What's wrong with that?"

"Moving on," his mother said. She still didn't say what Foster's problem was, but maybe it had to do with the fact West was ignoring half the emails his brother sent because he knew Foster had things under control and he didn't have time to deal with technology issues. "Elias has been trying to set up time to talk to you for months."

Elias was sibling number five. He owned a brewery in North Carolina and was thriving.

"Why is he going through you and not my assistant?" he asked.

"Maybe he feels as if he shouldn't have to go through your *assistant* to talk to his brother."

West wanted to pull his phone out to make a note like he was with Laken. "I'll call him too." He could do those things from his jet on the way back. "What's Rowan's issue?"

Rowan lived in Long Beach and ran a business making custom surfboards and accessories.

If anyone was living the perfect calm life, it was child number six at just twenty-six years old.

"He hasn't said too much to me," his mother admitted. "Nothing more than he hasn't had any communication directly with you in almost five months. It's all Braylon or Laken. Or through your assistant."

"No way," he said. It couldn't be that long since he'd even texted or emailed his brother.

"Yes," his mother said. "He's only been running the business for less than two years."

"I was told everything is going well," he said.

"It sounds it. Don't you think you should still check in rather than mentor or walk away after a few months and let other people handle him? Again, he's family."

Rowan would be added to the list now. That was three calls he had to make. "Nelson is the last of them. I mean I just had it out with Talia. She's got another month of school and then she knows she has to figure out what she wants and needs and we'll go from there."

That was what he did with all his siblings. He found a place for them somewhere. Nothing was free. They had to work for it, but he'd give them all sorts of chances and opportunities.

"Nelson is working things out. He needs guidance from you. You know he looks up to you more than the rest."

At twenty-four years old, Nelson was the youngest of the boys and had finished his MBA last year.

His brother thought he was going to jump into a leadership role and be a boss. Yep, he had another thing coming. He'd put his brother in one of his first companies and had him being mentored there.

He'd heard nothing but good things so far but hadn't seen Nelson in a while since he was in Virginia.

"He's doing great," he argued.

"I'm sure on a professional level he is. But it could be he needs to hear it from his big brother. Maybe he could spend some time with you."

"I'll see what I can do," he said. "Is that all?"

"No," his mother said. "You need a vacation. Right now.

Family first and you're putting them last. Your father would be disappointed."

His mother knew how to hit below the belt. "I've spent my life doing everything for our family."

"That's right," his mother said. "You're a wonderful person. You've shouldered so much and didn't need to. Everyone appreciates it. But you need to put yourself first at this point in order to see your siblings as family and not an obligation."

"I don't do that," he argued.

"West, you haven't seen or talked to half of them in so long that you probably couldn't even tell me if any of them were single or not."

He snorted. "That's their business, not mine."

"West! Family first. You may pull the purse strings, but I still run this family. I'm ordering you to take a week off. I know you won't stop working, but go to some island and get away. Put on a pair of shorts and get out of your damn suits."

He had jeans and a button-down shirt on right now. "I don't wear suits all the time."

To him a suit meant a tie and he didn't wear one unless he was in a meeting to acquire something. Most times he was in pants, a shirt and a jacket.

"It's eighty-five degrees here and you're in jeans. Loosen up. It will do you good to go away. You and I both know you can get a place with one or two phone calls."

"I don't have time for this crap."

"I talked to your assistant. She told me there is nothing scheduled for the next two weeks that can't wait or that you can't handle being away from town."

"You did what?" Talk about going behind his back.

"You heard me. As much as everyone is afraid of you, they are afraid of your mother too."

She wasn't lying. More so with that sweet smile on her face while she lectured him rather than his threat to lecture her as he'd said to Talia before his sister took off. She was the smart one of the day.

"I'm not taking a vacation."

"Want to test me and see who comes out on top?" his mother asked, her arms crossed. Oh boy, she looked like she did when most of the kids were fighting at once.

"You won't win," he said, smiling.

"We'll see about that."

2

GREAT ADVENTURE

Abby Sherman walked around the little bungalow she'd be staying at for a week.

How she won this trip, she'd never know.

She'd never won anything before in her life. Never even tried to win anything.

But her sister, Liz, and she entered this contest online for fun. Liz had been hoping to surprise her new fiancé, Christian Butler, with a trip.

For Abby, she just wanted to get away to a nice warm place she'd always dreamed of but could never afford.

And maybe it came at the right time when she felt she was burning out with frustration at work.

Not that she should be burned out at just twenty-seven years old in a career, but it felt it at times.

Too much gossip and petty crap from not only coworkers but employees too. She just wanted to do her job and go home, but it rarely happened without her playing referee.

Her phone rang and she walked over to her purse on the wicker table, fished it out and saw it was Liz calling.

"Hello," she said.

"You got there okay?" Liz asked.

"I landed about an hour ago, got my luggage and a cab and was brought to my bungalow. I'm not sure I want to ever leave this place." She knew her smile was filling her face.

"I want lots of pictures," Liz said. "Maybe I'll suggest the resort to Christian for our honeymoon."

"You've got time yet," she said. They hadn't even set a date yet, but she was positive it wouldn't be long.

"I do," Liz said. "Is the sun shining there? At least there is no snow here, but it's only fifty and kind of dreary."

"It is shining and it's eighty. The first thing I did was change into shorts and put my clothes away."

"I'm sorry you ended up going alone," Liz said.

"It was only for a single ticket," she said. They'd both put in for a vacation for two, but Abby also tried for the solo one.

"I know," Liz said. "Christian told me to go with you. He'd buy the ticket and we could have stayed together."

"It's fine," she said. "I know how hard it is for you to get time off of work."

Her sister was an ER nurse and, with a shortage of nurses, getting a week off on that short notice when it wasn't an emergency wasn't an easy thing.

"Think of it as a great adventure," Liz said.

"That is exactly what I'm doing," she said. "You picked up and moved and started a whole new life. This is just one week."

"Please don't compare the two," Liz said, laughing. "We know how well that turned out."

Her sister had moved to Georgia years ago with a friend. She'd met her ex-husband there and Tanner turned out to be abusive. Abby had kept that secret with her sister for years. Her older sister didn't want their father to know and worry.

But then one day Liz just returned home out of the blue and it was for the best.

A year after, her older sister reconnected with her old high school boyfriend and now they were engaged to be married.

That happy ever after that Abby wondered if she'd ever get.

The fairytale life she'd dreamed of as a child when she played with her dolls.

She'd have to find someone she could trust and believe in for that. Someone who wouldn't abandon her and break her heart.

Yeah, she knew she had Mommy issues and those things were just hard to let go of, no matter how much she tried.

"I'd say right now you had a roundabout way of it turning out just about perfect."

Liz laughed on the other line. "You're right. Speaking of perfect, he just walked in the door."

"Tell Christian I said hi," she said. "I'll let you go since I know you want to spend time with him before work."

Her sister worked third shift and most likely just got up before she called.

It was close to five thirty and Abby was starving. She'd spent most of the day in airports and only eating small snacks rather than a meal.

This trip was going to be a lot of firsts for her, but it was about experiencing life and enjoying this time away.

She picked up the map to see where everything was at the villa she was staying at. There were about twenty bunga-lows like the one she had, a few other bigger ones. There were all sorts of pools and activities to do, restaurants and spas.

This was an all-inclusive trip if she ate at the few places on the villa. She'd probably do that and just sign her name to the room where it'd be included. It's not like she wouldn't spend money here, but she could get away with spending very little if she didn't leave the villa.

A week of relaxing on the beach with some books sounded perfect to her.

She found the restaurant she decided to check out, then changed into a sundress and sandals. Might as well go in that way just in case shorts weren't appropriate. The dress was just as comfortable.

Her little crossbody purse flung over her shoulder, she tipped her head upside down, her long light brown hair with blonde streaks almost touching the floor as she ran her fingers through it to fluff it some.

Her makeup was light and in good shape when she checked in the mirror, so she made the short walk to get some food.

Along the path, she discovered where a lot of things were, made some mental notes and would spend more time checking out the grounds in the morning.

The last thing she wanted to do was walk alone at night. Her father was already worried as it was, but she'd texted him right away when she landed and then talked to him on the way to the villa.

She'd even texted her mother, who had recently entered their lives again.

Abby had been hurt so many times by her mother that she was being more guarded, but it didn't mean she couldn't say she landed safely.

When she got to the hostess station, they asked if she

wanted a table or to sit at the bar. She opted for the bar so as to not take a table from someone else.

She was placed on the side and that worked out well with her back to the wall and she could see into the room. She liked to people watch.

"What can I get you to drink?" the bartender asked.

She looked at the menu of drinks he'd put in front of her. They all had exotic names and mixtures of fruits and rum. She didn't want to look like a fool and not pronounce something right.

"A Malibu sunset sounds like it'd hit the spot," she said. All the flavors she liked even if she'd never had the drink before.

"Coming right up," the bartender said. "Are you eating or just having a drink?"

"I'd like to order dinner too, please."

The bartender smiled. "And she has such sweet manners to go with her looks."

Abby grinned. She'd been told she was too sweet at times. She didn't think it was an insult, but maybe it was meant to be.

She worked in HR for a local major grocery chain. It felt as if HR was hated by everyone. But most liked her and it could be because she tried to almost be apologetic with every conversation she had.

She wasn't one for confrontations if she could avoid them. She didn't get mad. She tried not to get upset even though everyone told her she wore her heart on her sleeve.

She just did what needed to be done and tried to ruffle as few feathers as possible.

"Thank you," she said when he handed her the menu.

She scanned it quickly while her drink was being made. When it was placed in front of her, she pointed to the fish special. Again, couldn't pronounce it and didn't want to be laughed at.

Too many times in her life she was talked about.

The girl whose mother was in and out of mental institutions and rehab facilities.

Her father had raised her and her sister alone and he'd done a darn good job of it. At times, her sister took on raising her and, looking back, Abby might not have appreciated it as much as she should have.

Though she was jealous of everything Liz had in life right now, she was thrilled for her sister too.

She sipped her drink and looked around at all the couples. Everyone seemed happy to be here. She couldn't blame them. She was too, except she wished that she had a man next to her for a trip like this.

An hour later, with her drink gone and her dinner plate almost empty, the bartender came over and placed another drink down.

"From the gentleman at the table over there," the bartender said.

She turned her head to where the man was pointed out. Looked like someone in their early thirties.

"Thank you," she said. "But I didn't want another drink. Could you decline for me?"

The bartender shook his head at the man who had ordered the drink. The guy looked like he was going to pout but nodded his head.

"Can I get you something else?"

"How about a club soda," she said.

The bartender laughed. She did want a drink, but not another one filled with that much rum. Getting drunk on her first night here, all alone. Yep, that would be stupid.

Her club soda was placed down and she finished up her

dinner. It was way too good to not. "Would you like dessert?" the bartender asked.

Might as well since she got a fresh drink. She glanced at the small menu and decided on a slice of coconut cake. It'd go well with the rest of the meal.

"What's a pretty thing like you doing here all by yourself?"

Abby turned to see the man who had the drink sent over to her standing there. Moving forward, he took the seat by her. He crowded in close when he did it, his arm brushing against her.

"Having dinner," she said.

"But you didn't want another drink?" the guy asked. "I'm Liam, by the way."

She didn't offer her name. "No, I was done drinking for the night," she said politely. "Just going to finish my dessert and go back."

"It's a beautiful spot to vacation, isn't it?" Liam asked.

She didn't want to say she was on vacation, but she was pretty sure the guy wouldn't think she was a local.

"It is," she said. Might as well be agreeable. She'd done this enough in her job. The last thing she wanted was more attention on her.

Liam held his hand up for another beer after draining his. "I'm here with some buddies for the week," he said. "Maybe we can get to know each other more."

She felt her face pale and wondered how she was going to get out of this.

Saying she wasn't alone wasn't the thing to do. What if he saw her around by herself?

She didn't want to make a scene here either.

Liam was leaning in really close, much closer in her

personal space than she wanted anyone to be, and she knew her back was arching to get away.

"There you are, sweetie. I've been looking for you. Sorry I got held up on a call." Abby turned her head to see a man in tan shorts and a white fitted T-shirt move over. He slipped his arm around her, his beard tickling her ear, and as he leaned in to kiss her cheek, he whispered, "Play along."

Oh shit. She was in trouble and she knew it.

3

SORROW AND REGRET

West walked into the restaurant prepared to get a beer and burger. If he could find anything on the island that resembled real beef.

He had every intention of staying in his room and working like he'd been doing most of the day.

How his mother guilted him into this damn trip, he'd be asking himself for years to come.

He'd still be in his bungalow if his mother didn't call and tell him to get his ass outside and come back with a tan.

There was only one woman he ever really listened to and it was his mother.

Two days ago, he'd flown back home after he got the biggest lecture of his life. Manipulated into even showing up there.

That burned more than anything, that he actually fell for it.

He talked to those three of his siblings, then felt like shit that he'd been ignoring them when they all had important things to discuss.

One being a gift for their mother's birthday.

After he'd spoken to three of his siblings, he called the rest and apologized for being distant.

They all seemed stunned and blown away by his apology, as if they didn't expect him to give it, and it made him realize he needed time away to think.

Being an asshole was never the kind of person he was and he didn't know how it happened.

He called his assistant, whom he paid heavily to do these things last minute for him, she found a place, set up his jet and all he did was show up for the takeoff.

When he saw the lovely young woman at the bar getting hit on and the panicked look on her face, he did the same thing he'd do if it were one of his sisters.

He swooped in to save the day with the fastest line he could think of. It probably came off as a pickup line too but nothing he could do about it now.

The way her body stiffened, he realized his tactic might have just scared her more.

"I didn't know she was taken," the dude hitting on the cute blonde said.

"She is," he said. "Maybe you should find another woman to chat up."

He had the dude by six inches and easily fifty pounds. Even if he didn't, he had his boardroom face in place. The one that commanded attention and respect with a look in his eyes.

The guy took off and he moved into the seat on the other side.

"Thanks," she said.

"You're welcome," he said. "I can get up and leave once he is gone. No worries. I don't mean any harm. Just saw a little of my younger sister in you."

"Oh," she said. "I wasn't sure."

"I could tell," he said. "Guess I could have approached it differently. Again, meant no harm. I came in for a burger and a beer."

She laughed. "Good luck finding that here. I find the menu caters heavily to fish. I might be nervous whether you get real beef or not."

He knew that. "One could hope. I'm West," he said, holding his hand out.

"West?" she asked. "Is your sister's name East?"

He grinned. Then was shocked he did that. He honestly couldn't remember the last time he smiled. He hadn't even thought of it until Laken pointed it out to him when they talked.

That the brother she grew up with had been fun and carefree. He used to smile and laugh.

Then when their father died, it was as if his joy did too.

Those words just slammed a hammer into his chest. The pain of it almost cracked a rib.

Sorrow and regret filled the hole the hammer left.

Had he lost so much of who he was trying to make his father proud?

It seemed as if he might have.

"No. That sister is Talia. The other is Laken."

"I've got a sister named Liz," she said. "Just one though. No brothers."

"Oh, I've got five brothers."

"Five," she said, her jaw dropping. "Your parents were busy."

He still had a grin on his face. "Yeah." Seemed like every time his father was home, he left their mother with more than hugs and kisses. Always another baby in the belly.

He remembered his father had only been home for Talia's birth of the eight kids. Sad when he thought of it. He never got to see Talia past four years old and even then, it was only about half her life.

No one got a lot of time with their father. Not even his mother.

"I bet you're the oldest."

"What makes you think that?" he asked.

"The take charge way you came in on the white horse. Then the way you tried to ease me after. As if you've been rounding up siblings and breaking up fights for years."

If she only knew. And she wouldn't know because he had no intention of telling her who he was or what his worth was.

"I am the oldest," he said. "You?"

"The baby," she said. "My sister is seven years older."

"I'm fourteen years older than Talia," he said.

"Then you must be old," she said, grinning at him.

Her light brown eyes were twinkling some and he was relaxing her enough that she didn't seem panicked that a stranger was talking to her at the bar.

When the bartender came over, he ordered his beer, looked at the menu placed in front of him quickly and then picked the fish special.

"Older than you for sure," he said.

"I had that for dinner. It's good."

"That's good to hear," he said. "Do you want another drink? I'm assuming that is club soda or seltzer."

"Club soda," she said. "I'll take another."

The bartender wasn't looking, but West lifted his hand, pointed to Abby's glass, she nodded and it was filled and put in front of her.

"Is there someone coming that I need to move over for?" he asked.

"Nope," she said. "You're good."

She didn't answer if she was here alone though. He wouldn't ask. That might scare her again.

"This is a nice place," he said.

Though he thought his bungalow was too small, Vanessa did good work for short notice.

There were no complaints about the view. His place was almost on a deck right on the water. All the bungalows were.

He was guessing Abby had the means to be here, because no way he'd stay at a place not up to his standards, and that cost money.

Not that he asked the cost and wouldn't. He had no reason to. Vanessa had his credit card and it'd be charged and paid for by the company.

"It is," she said. "I won the trip."

"You won it?" he asked. He didn't realize that was actually a thing. "Like on a game show?"

"No," she said. "My sister and I bought tickets for an online raffle. It was for a couple or single. I did both. I didn't know I was a runner up and when the winner of the single one couldn't make it, they called me. I was shocked. I had to make a quick decision and got the week off of work."

"Congrats then," he said.

"I've never won anything before. It was a shock. Now I'm here and wondering what to do."

She might not have realized she'd told him she was alone and he wouldn't point that out.

"I'm sure there is lots to do here."

"What about you?" she asked. "What do you plan on doing? Or are you going to work?"

"What makes you think I was working?" he asked.

"I don't think you're the type to lie. Though your actions with me were fibbing, you didn't outright lie about anything.

You said hi and that you were sorry you were held up on the phone. My guess is you were."

She was good. "I am. Kind of a working vacation," he admitted.

"That's too bad that your employer can't give you the time off. We all need a break at times."

"We do," he said. "I'll take some of it off. Maybe it's not fun doing things alone."

She grinned. "So if you had someone to do things with you'd take a break?"

He thought of all the things he had going on and then told himself that maybe they could wait.

He had a lot of competent people working for him. Including his siblings. They could reach him if need be.

"Yeah," he said. "I would. Not to put any pressure on you or anything."

"No pressure," she said. "I'm not a very trusting person so don't take offense if I change my mind."

"No worries," he said. "I understand." Even if he knew he'd be disappointed.

He couldn't remember the last time he'd been disappointed in anything in life.

For the past decade he got what he wanted when he wanted it.

No one told him no.

It was unheard of.

He didn't think he was a bully though. But maybe many thought it.

"The fact you said that makes me want to give you a chance. So where are you from?" she asked. "I know your first name."

"Carlisle," he said. "That's my last name." He wouldn't lie and the name was common enough. The last name was. It's not like he thought she'd do a Google search on him.

If she did, she'd find out fast who he really was, but again, he'd go on the hope she was just looking for some companionship for her time here.

West was a good judge of character and something told him Abby wouldn't be the type to see dollar signs and then change her mind on what she was looking for.

"Sherman," she said. "That's my last name."

"You asked where I was from. I'm from a lot of places. I'm an Army brat. I live in Manhattan right now."

"Goes with the important job," she said. "Big city living. Funny how we are both in New York. I'm in Colonie though. Just outside of Albany."

"I'm familiar with the area," he said. Not that he'd been there personally, but Albany was the capital of New York. He'd talked to the governor a few times, and even been invited to the capital. Politicians were always trying to hit him up for contributions.

"Small world," she said.

"It can be," he said.

His dinner was put down in front of him at the same time as her dessert.

She picked up her fork and sliced it through the white cake with toasted coconut coating it. There was a drizzle of chocolate on the outside of it.

He tried not to watch as she put it in her mouth, her eyes closing in delight. "This is better than the dinner. I love dessert but don't eat it much. I'll have to make sure I do a lot of walking while I'm here to not gain any weight."

He couldn't tell much from her body with her sitting down other than she was wearing a long summer dress and she had to be a little taller.

Her arms were toned, so he felt she had to be in decent shape.

He tried his fish. "This is pretty good," he said. "Not sure beer is the right choice with it."

"I had a Malibu sunset. Coconut rum and pineapple and orange juice. It went well."

"Sounds sweet to me," he said. "Kind of like you."

"I'm told that a lot," she said.

"Why did you frown?"

"I think it's my job. I mean, I'm nice and professional. I work in HR."

"One of the most hated departments out there," he said, grinning. At least he'd heard it enough. His HR staff were feared and he understood the reason. Most bad news was delivered through them.

"It is. I work a lot in hiring and retention and policies for a large grocery chain. It's hard to find staffing, more so part-timers. Then trying to find out what we can do to keep them aside from more money."

"Money isn't the only way to keep staff," he said.

"I know that. But when they aren't making much, that is all they think of. I also focus on policies and trust me when I tell you that people hate to follow the rules."

He grinned. "I know."

"I bet you're a rule maker. Maybe even a breaker."

She still didn't come out and ask him what he did. He wouldn't volunteer, but there were all sorts of things he could say and nothing would be a lie.

"I do both," he said. "Depends when or where it's called for."

"Okay, I've got to know. You aren't saying what you do. You don't have to tell me, I get it."

He felt bad. She was being a good sport. Not even pushy.

"You could say I'm a fixer. I do what needs to be done when it needs to be done."

"That I believe," she said. "Just like you fixed this situation with that jerk earlier. And that would explain why you need a break and should take time off of work. Fixing other people's problems is depressing and stressful. You might even absorb that negativity yourself. That's why I needed this trip. I felt like I was the sponge wiping up everyone's moods and it was affecting my own."

She was pretty smart for someone who seemed young.

"That's some good insight," he said. "Guess maybe I should listen to you and find some things to do to relax since I'm here."

"That's the spirit," she said.

4

HER LITTLE SECRET

Abby changed her bathing suit one more time the next day. She'd brought three with her and the third was going to be her choice. It was more of an athletic piece and would work for what was planned. She grabbed another sundress and slipped that over her suit while she put some clothes in a bag to change into later on.

Somehow she was going snorkeling with a sexy man that she met less than twenty-four hours ago.

One that saved the day, you could say.

Then rather than just thank him and walk away, she was going to put a swimsuit on and dive into the ocean looking at fish with him.

She might be crazy, but it's not like she was going to be alone with him.

They'd sat at the bar for an hour longer than it took for West to finish his meal, then he walked her back to her bungalow. He was only two down. He'd even offered to go to his first so she didn't think he was following her.

She found it funny and sweet at the same time and said it was okay.

It's not like she was going to tell her father what she was doing. He'd jump on the next plane and come try to talk her out of it.

She wanted to tell her sister, but Liz would be sleeping. She'd lost her window to call when she knew Liz would be getting out of work.

There was part of her that was so giddy with excitement that she had to share it, then the other part that thought it was best to let it be her little secret for now.

She could relay it as something she did and he was on the boat with her. There'd be more than just the two of them.

West had asked her what she wanted to do while she was here and she honestly hadn't put much thought into anything other than relaxing on the beach. But she wanted to spend time with him and she knew beyond a doubt, he wasn't the type to sit and do nothing.

Not that she knew all that much about him other than his pale skin said he didn't get out much.

She got a feeling about him and she was going with it.

Could be more the fact he was attractive, had a way about him that demanded attention, yet was considerate too.

It was as if he knew he made her nervous at first and then tried to counter that.

When she heard a knock at her bungalow door, she rushed to open it and saw West standing there. He had navy swim trunks on that hit him past mid thigh, another fitted T-shirt, this time orange. The color looked fabulous on him.

"Come in," she said.

"It's not too early?" he asked. "I've been up for a while."

"Probably working," she said.

"Things need to get done," he said. He was smirking at her and she wasn't sure what to make of that.

"You're a workaholic, aren't you?"

"It's been said more than once," he said drily.

She'd ignore that for now. It's not like she needed or demanded his time.

He was a stranger in a location at the same time as her. They were going to have some fun today and maybe she'd never see him again.

Abby hated that thought that popped into her head, but it was there. It's not like she was the vacation fling type of person, nor was she out trying to find her forever love.

If it wasn't for Liz and Christian's relationship recently, she wasn't sure she could say she even believed in happy ever after.

It's not like she'd witnessed it with her parents. Her father never even tried to move on.

All she ever had in her head were things she read about, saw on TV or dreamed her life could be like.

"No one can say that about me," she said. "But I do put a lot of hours in. I try to disconnect at the end of the day. I mean, I don't check my email or anything. Once in a while I'll get a text, but it's nice that so many things are above my pay grade."

"People normally say that so they don't have to do that work," he said.

"True. I say it more so that I don't have to stress about it. It's not like I've got much decision-making power and am not sure I want it. Is that horrible of me?"

"Not at all," he said. "Not everyone can lead. Not everyone can be the one to make a decision. But you did decide on today. Unless you want to change your mind."

She giggled at the way he'd said that. Like he was confused and didn't want to push.

"Nope," she said. "Once I make up my mind I don't change it often. This did sound fun and if I didn't have someone to do it with, I'm not sure I would have pushed myself."

"Why?" he asked.

She shrugged. "It's hard for me to get out of my comfort zone at times."

"Maybe we can talk some more about that today," he said. "Me, I'm not sure what my comfort zone is."

"Considering you said you were an army brat, you've moved a lot, right? And you've got so many siblings. Nothing was probably ever calm in your house."

"No," he said simply. "You?"

"My father tried. He's the best. But things happen that are beyond anyone's control."

"Tell me about it," he said. "What was it for you? Or is that too personal?"

She slipped her sandals on, grabbed her bag and put it over her shoulder. Her purse was across her body too.

West took her bag for her. She found that sweet. Not many men seemed to have manners anymore.

"I'll tell you something personal if you tell me something."

"Sure," he said.

"My mother left when I was four. She came back in and out of my life a lot, disrupting it. I didn't understand the full extent of everything until I was older."

"What was there to understand?" he asked.

"She has severe bipolar. My father tried to get her help, but she didn't want it. She was in and out of rehab because she self-medicated with drugs and alcohol. I'm not sure why I'm saying this to you."

"Because even though you say you don't trust people easily, you know I won't judge you," he said.

"Maybe," she said. "I guess I could be just telling you some of why I don't trust easily either."

"Do you still have contact with your mother?" he asked.

"She's back in the area again. She's in another group home and doing well. I'm holding out hope that maybe this is the time she gets better, but I know that doesn't mean much. So yes, we are in contact and things are going well, but it's only been four months too."

He nodded his head and they started to walk away from the bungalows. She expected a taxi to be there, but he was holding a door to a Mercedes.

"I don't like to rely on others when I need to go somewhere," he said.

"This does make it easier," she said. "As long as you don't get us lost."

"That is what the navigation system is for. I already put the address in."

"Because you're efficient like that," she said, smiling.

"You make that sound like it's a bad trait," he said, climbing in behind the wheel.

"Not at all. I like to think I live that way too. Sometimes you just have to."

There was silence after she said that and she was okay with it. He was focusing on getting them out of the parking lot.

If her eyes were on his hands as he moved the wheel and backed out, she wouldn't let on. He had some big hands on him. Feet too.

Oh my, her body was flushing without her being able to

control it.

"My father died when I was in high school. Right before my eighteenth birthday. Talia, the sister I said you remind me of, was four at the time too."

That statement broke through the air like a balloon exploding.

"I'm so sorry," she said. "Was he in the service when it happened?"

"Yes," he said. "Overseas. He was transporting supplies to other countries and their plane was shot down."

Her hand went in front of her mouth. "Did they...never mind."

"They did recover the bodies. If they hadn't, I think my mother would have never believed it."

"I don't know if I could have either," she said.

Now she knew why he seemed to be in control at all times. He had to have stepped up to be the father figure for all his siblings.

"My mother was heartbroken. We all were. I hadn't seen him for eight months. We talked on the phone more than anything. He called my mother all the time, spoke to us weekly, but you know, it's not the best life."

"You have to be a strong woman to be married to a man in the service," she said.

"You're right. Just like your father had to be strong to raise two daughters and deal with what was surely a stressful situation in your household."

"He is a strong man. The greatest. Liz was like a mother to me too. I guess I feel as if I'll never be able to repay her."

"Why do you have to?" he asked.

"Because she has or had her own demons and when she should have been acting like a kid she was helping to raise me while my father was working. He owns his own fencing company. Certain times of the year the days are long and hard."

"Guess being raised by a single parent is something we've got in common," she said.

"We do," he said.

"And now we can talk about fun things. I'm not a bag full of drama and don't want you to think that."

She'd had enough men in her life that she'd dated that had said that to her. Liz had the same problem too with her ex-husband.

"I don't know you enough to think that," he said.

He didn't say anything about wanting to know more either. That was fine. She was going back to her quiet life and he was going back to an exciting one she was sure.

But why couldn't they have today? Or this week?

No one was saying they couldn't.

Wasn't life worth living?

"Nope," she said. "The same with you. Maybe that is what makes this so much easier. No expectations."

"Is that what you're looking for?" he asked, frowning at her.

"I'm not asking for much. Are you? I just met you."

"That works for me," he said.

He was smiling again.

"That doesn't mean we are going to have sex," she said.

"I don't believe I asked."

"But you wouldn't fight me off if I offered," she said.

"Do I come across as stupid to you?" he asked, smirking.

"You come across as a man who knows what he wants and makes sure he gets it," she said, grinning.

"Then we understand each other well."

Guess that would be considered somewhat of a mic drop by him.

5

COOL AND SOPHISTICATED

West wasn't sure what made him say what he had, but it came out of his mouth before he could hit pause and rewind.

Since Abby only smiled, he was going to assume she didn't take offense to it.

He was too busy worrying about the way his body was going to react when he saw her in a swimsuit today.

Another one of those sundresses was hiding her body and something told him it was going to be a treat to look at when it came off.

He found the boat they'd be getting on fast enough, parked his rental and they got out.

"You can leave your purse and bag in here if you want," he said. "That's up to you."

"I don't want to lose anything. I don't need my phone on me. I don't think."

There was uncertainty in her voice and face and he didn't want her to have that.

He thought again if this were his sister he'd be flipping out if she did that with a stranger.

"Why don't you bring your phone with you? Do you have a pocket in your dress?"

"I do," she said. "Thanks. Never know when you might need to call for help."

"That's right," he said. "The rest of our phones might die because we didn't charge them the night before."

"Again, I don't think you ever let yourself get into any situation where you aren't the one in control."

He found it funny she pegged him so well for not knowing him.

Was he that easy to read?

Must be if his family all ganged up on him with his mother and she managed to get him on this trip.

Or maybe it was more that his mother knew he'd have so much guilt over his actions and unawareness that he'd do it to try to self-reflect.

"You just never know," he said. "I could be distracted by a beautiful blonde with long legs."

"Might be one on the boat. I'm not blonde."

He reached for a lock of her hair and let the silken feel of it drop between his fingers. "This piece is blonde."

"Highlights," she said. "I treated myself to them when I found out about the trip."

"They look nice on you."

"Only nice?" she said, flipping her hair to one side playfully.

He liked that she was warming up even when she was being cautious.

"More than like, but you know, I can't come on too strong."

"Then I'll say I like the beard on you. It's kind of unkempt and I bet it's new for you."

His hand went up and he scratched the itchy hair on his face.

He rarely went more than two days without shaving, but he was here and trying not to be found out for who he was.

Not that he thought anyone would recognize him, but why take that chance?

"I don't normally have one this long," he admitted. "But it is supposed to be a vacation."

"Then we are both doing things a little differently."

He didn't think he was. He paid for this adventure today even though Abby argued. He figured it was the least he could do since she was getting him away from work. He wasn't sure any woman had argued with him before not to pay for something.

"Here's to some fun in the sun," he said.

They walked to the boat, gave their name and were told there were five more people on the way. Once everyone was there, they'd get instructions on what to do and how to put the equipment on.

"You do know how to swim, right?" she asked. "You're pasty white like me."

He laughed. "I do," he said. "I swim regularly for exercise."

He had a lap pool in his penthouse. Not a big one but one that allowed him to swim against a current.

Abby didn't need to know that though.

"I haven't swum in a while. I did a lot as a kid. I had friends with pools. I spent two years on the swim team, but it wasn't my thing. I guess I was trying different things. I was more girly and not into other sports like my sister."

"If I was to guess, I'd say you were a cheerleader or did gymnastics?"

"Cheerleader," she said. "I was the girl playing house

with her Barbies for years. I wasn't one to go out and sweat much. This way you can be cool when you work out."

"Do you still work out?" he asked. It would explain the toned arms.

"Not often. I'm on the skinny side. My sister, Liz, she's buff."

"Buff?" he asked.

"Well, not really. She's shorter than me. She's an ER nurse. She was really thin too but started to work out and got strong. She needs it in her job. I'm jealous but not as disciplined as her. You know, that sweating thing."

"No sweating today," he said. "Just relaxing."

As he'd said those words, the rest of the people came up on the boat and they were given all the instructions and then the boat set sail.

They didn't go that far out, they could still see the land, but then started to put their fins on. He pulled his shirt off, and Abby did the same with her dress. She'd set her dress next to his shirt in a locker to keep their phones safe.

He had all he could do not to let drool flow out of his mouth when she turned her back in the aqua bikini. No one would think he was cool and sophisticated now with the wood he was trying not to sport.

Her suit was the athletic kind. The top was like a sports bra and she was rather small, but it went with the rest of her body. Her legs were long for her height, which he was guessing was about five foot five.

She was thin and it had been hidden well under those sundresses she'd been wearing.

"What?" she asked.

"Huh?"

"You're staring," she said. She moved closer. "One might think we just met."

"You're staring too," he said, laughing.

"I happen to like what I see."

"The same," he said.

He couldn't wait to hit the water. He felt like a thirteen-year-old boy at an older sister's pool party with all her friends.

"Then we have more in common," she said.

She finished getting her equipment on, then walked to the edge and jumped in. He did the same and the two of them started swimming side by side on the surface of the water, just testing out the snorkeling equipment and making sure they could breathe well enough with it.

Then she dove and he followed.

There was no talking and they didn't need to.

She reached out and grabbed his hand, then pointed to the school of colored fish.

After a minute, she surfaced for some air.

"What's wrong?" he asked.

"I wish I had a camera that could take pictures underwater."

"Let's go back to the boat," he said.

"Are you done?"

"Nope. You can buy cameras. I should have done it. I'm going to shout to them to toss us one."

"You don't need to do that," she argued.

"Yes, I do. Got to have something other than my memories in my brain."

"That's sweet," she said. "Only if I can get some pictures of you in it."

"Then I need to get some of you in them too."

They got to the boat, West shouted up for a camera and swam closer to have it handed to him.

He snapped a picture of her quickly. A silly one. "The least you could do was let me remove the snorkel."

"We'll do that later," he said.

They swam back to where they were before, dove down and saw a bunch of fish. Abby was pointing to different things and he was taking the pictures.

They came back up and he handed it to her so she could snap some too.

They must have been swimming for over an hour and kicking around pointing and laughing and smiling. Not saying a word.

He wasn't sure he'd ever been around a man let alone a beautiful woman for so long without talking.

Nor did he do any activities with someone in the peace and quiet.

But here all they had was the sound of the water and waves. Some laughter from them both and their breathing.

It was by far the most calming hour of his life in the past ten years or more.

"I'm beat," she finally said. "And hungry. I wonder what they are serving us for lunch."

"Looks like the others are back there already. Hope they left us some."

The two of them swam back to the boat. He helped her up and tried not to groan when her ass was close to his face as she climbed up.

At least his body was cooled down.

She wrapped a towel around her, then he caught the one thrown at him.

"They've got sandwiches and fruit."

"Looks good to me," he said.

They both made a plate and found a seat in the sun on the deck to soak up some heat.

"This has been so much fun and it's not even over with. Thank you for doing it with me."

"You're welcome," he said. "Don't suppose there is a chance we can get some dinner tonight when we get back?"

"You mean you don't have to work for taking a few hours off?" she asked.

She was laughing at him. "I can get it done later," he said.

"I think dinner sounds great. I can go back and sit in the sun at my place and read while you work before dinner. No reason for you to get behind and then be thinking about that and stressing rather than paying attention to me."

"I'd never think about work over a beautiful woman," he said.

At least he didn't plan on that tonight.

The sad part was, he couldn't remember the last time he'd spent this much time with a woman and he knew there was no way he was blowing it thinking about someone or something else.

6

THE GOOD GIRL

Somehow Abby found herself sitting in the sun at West's bungalow instead of hers hours later.

Never would she have agreed to this back home so soon on a first date.

She wasn't back home. She was with a hot guy that made her blood boil and she was hoping she did the same for him.

He was classy and sophisticated. She could see it even in his casual clothing.

And he wanted her. Or wanted to spend time with her.

Most men like West didn't give her the time of day.

A girl with her upbringing of a single father, a mentally ill mother, working middle class.

Cinderella story...not likely.

They had a roof over their head and she went to college, but they never had a lot in life.

Or she didn't.

Liz had married a man with money and it didn't turn out so well.

This time around her sister was marrying a man for love

and the fact he had money was a bonus more than anything else.

Abby only wanted a man that saw her for who she was.

Who had the same dreams as her.

One that understood where she came from and where she was going.

"You're going to get a lopsided tan that way."

She turned her head from where she was sitting on a lounge. She was lying back at an angle, her Kindle that she never left the house without on her lap, big sunglasses on her face.

"What way?" she asked.

"Your front only," he said, coming to sit next to her in the other lounge. "How about your back?"

"I can't reach that with lotion."

He picked up the bottle and the can of spray on the little table. "Turn over if you want."

"If you don't mind." She flipped over for him.

He laughed. A deep sound that almost vibrated in his chest and sent all sorts of tingles in every part of her body that was covered with her bathing suit.

"Not at all. What would you have done if you were alone?" he asked. "Not get any sun on your back?"

"I would have tried to spray as much as I could and hope for no burns."

"No reason to hope for anything," he said.

She put her Kindle down on the wood of the deck. Then turned in the chair so her head was facing the ocean rather than her feet. She'd be able to see the water through the seams of the decking. It was awesome being right over the ocean the way they were.

Last night there was a tiny fear that a big storm might

send her crashing a few feet down, but she finally fell asleep to the sounds of nature around her.

Nothing like the apartment complex she lived in.

She heard the lotion being squirted on West's hands. She'd been hoping he was going to spray her down.

The minute his big hands landed on her shoulders and started to rub it in she had to fight hard to not let out a groan.

He laughed again and she was positive he was aware of her dilemma.

"Did you cover everything?" she asked when his hands were around her waist and lower back.

Then a few fingers slipped under the waistband. "Just want to make sure in case your suit moves."

"Better safe than sorry," she said.

He put more lotion on his hands and then went to the bottom of her feet and up her calves, behind her knees, her hamstrings.

She held her breath wondering what he'd do when he got close to her butt.

She didn't have to wait long.

He did the same thing as he had to her waist. Slipped his fingers under to "just to be safe."

"Better?" he asked.

"Oh yeah," she said softly.

"Sorry, I'm not much company right now."

"It's fine," she said. "I know you're a busy man."

"You do?" he asked. He sounded confused. "How is that?"

"You look it. I said that before. Not to mention you're on vacation and working so that must mean you need to do that. Most people don't if they can avoid it."

"Things need to get done," he said. "I'm the only one

that can at times."

"See," she said. "Important too."

This time it was a forced laugh. "I've been told that too."

"Go back to work then," she said. "Earn your money for this trip. I'm glad I won it. I'd never be able to stay in a place like this. Ever. It's once in a lifetime and I'm going to enjoy it until Friday."

"You're leaving on Friday?" he asked.

"Yes. Not that long. Four nights and kind of five days. It's fine. I'll need the weekend to put myself back in work mode. What about you? You didn't say how much longer you were here?"

She hoped it was more than a few days.

"Friday too," he said.

"I'd ask if we were on the same plane, but I doubt it. Maybe leaving. But then I'll go to Albany Airport and you're going to..."

"JFK," he said.

"Then we've got a few days if we want. Or just today."

She wanted more time but wouldn't be the one to say that. As she mentioned, he was busy.

"I do want more," he said.

She read the double meaning there.

Though she wanted to push it aside, she wouldn't.

She'd always been the good girl. Or she tried to be. As she got older she knew how much her father had sacrificed for her and Liz and she'd tried to never draw eyes to her family. Or more than what was there.

But no one was here.

No one would know if she had a fling.

She wouldn't do it tonight. No way.

A few more days. Might be best to just play things out.

"It's nice to want things," she said, laughing.

She heard the top close down on the lotion, then it was set down next to her.

"I came out to see if you wanted a drink or anything. It's only three. Not sure when you wanted to go to dinner. Lots of places or we could order in."

"Ordering in sounds fun if you're willing to talk some."

"Talk about what?" he asked.

She shrugged and turned to look at him, putting her chin in her hand, leaning on her elbow.

"Life," she said. "Maybe just get to know each other more. My life is so boring. Yours has to be exciting. You've traveled and I haven't."

"You're traveling now," he said.

"Because I won it," she said. "Not the same thing."

"It's not," he said. "But dinner in sounds very doable in my eyes. You didn't answer if you wanted a drink or a snack?"

"If you've got some water, that would be good."

He left before she could say anything else and she hung her arms over the side of the chair to hold onto her Kindle as she read with her head down.

When she felt an ice-cold droplet on her back she let out a screech and he laughed.

"Feel good?" he asked.

"It did," she said. "I might have to take a dip to cool off at some point. You could take a break and join me if you want."

"I think I will before we order dinner."

His bare feet moved silently back inside. He had the doors open and she could hear him talking from time to time, but decided to grab her phone and put some music on.

She didn't want him to think she was listening in.

As much as she'd like to know more about his job, she really didn't.

It wouldn't mean much to her and it's not like she had any grand plans after Friday.

Those would be crazy thoughts in her mind and she tried to keep them to a minimum.

Long-distance relationships were never anything she'd want in her life. You can't get to know someone well if you don't see them much.

She'd seen traditional from afar her whole life and that was what she thought of when she imagined her future.

Before she put her phone down, she snapped some pictures and sent them to Liz.

She hadn't expected her sister to call her and hesitated just a moment before she answered.

Liz would have no idea that she wasn't in her own bungalow.

"I'm so jealous," Liz said. "I wish now that I'd called in sick for the week."

Abby laughed. "You'd never do that and you know it."

"I've done it before but not for a week."

Her sister had called into her job in the past when she was married because her controlling ex-husband forced it.

"No need to do it now. I'm sure Christian would take you here if you ask. You need to think about it. Maybe your honeymoon for sure."

Christian wouldn't spare any cost. She knew that too.

"If he sees these pictures it won't take much convincing," Liz said. "What did you do on your first day there? Just relax and take in the sun?"

"I went snorkeling," she said. "It was so much fun. I'll send you some pictures I took on the boat."

"Jealous again," Liz said. "And I'm thrilled you're spending some money and doing fun things."

"I was worried a bit, but I told myself I won't have

another chance to do this."

No reason she'd say that West paid for it. She wasn't happy but it's not like it was all that much money.

She'd given herself a five-hundred-dollar budget to spend while she was here. That was generous in her eyes, knowing all her food would be covered if she stayed in the villas.

Her father slipped her a few hundred this weekend too because he didn't want her to not experience something fearing the credit card bill when she returned.

It's not that she was poor. She wasn't.

She had a good job and made decent money. But she lived alone, had some student loans, a car loan, other bills and things added up fast.

No reason to go nuts and come home with a massive credit card bill that she'd struggle to pay.

"That's right," Liz said. "You'd never go crazy. Ever. But enjoy it. Really. If anyone deserves this, it's you."

"Thanks, Liz. I guess I needed to hear that."

"You work so hard. You're so nice and polite and take a ton of bullshit from people at your job. This is a great reward for all your work and think of it that way."

She turned her head and saw West walking around with the phone to his ear. She couldn't hear what he was saying. Not with talking to Liz and the music going.

"Yeah," she said. "Time to reward myself like never before."

Her eyes were traveling the length of his body. His shirt was off, his bathing suit still on and he was barefoot. He had some serious muscles on him for a guy that seemed to work in an office.

When her body heated up, she turned back to look at the water and hoped it cooled her off some for now.

7

MAKE THAT MOVE

Two hours later, West was out on the deck.

His shirt was off, the towel on the chair and he was diving into the water to swim by her.

He could or should have been doing more work, but he had a sexy woman in his eyesight who wasn't demanding much of his time and he'd be nuts to ignore her.

Maybe the fact she wasn't demanding his time and doing her own thing made him feel comfortable enough to let her come back here and relax.

She'd hesitated, but she could have left and returned to hers two down at any point.

"This is refreshing," he said when he came up for air. Abby was treading water next to where he'd swum out. His feet could touch the bottom of the soft sand.

"It is," she said. "And better than taking a shower. I always have to get all the lotion off of me, but I can rub it off in the water."

"Need some help with that?" he asked, wiggling his eyebrows.

She held her arm up and ran one hand down it. "I can do the front again, but the back is kind of tricky."

He reached forward and pulled her close so that she was plastered against the front of him while his hand moved up and down her back and shoulders.

She was laughing and he joined in, his fingers dipping into the edge of the waist of her bikini bottoms like they had when he applied the lotion.

It took Herculean strength not to cup her ass and pull her next to his groin.

"No problem with this?" he asked as his hands moved some more.

"No," she said. "Do you have a problem with it?"

He snorted. "Not at all."

She lifted her head up, her eyes looking into his. He figured he had her wet body plastered against him, his hands on her back, he might as well go in for a kiss.

He dipped his head, she inched up and their lips met.

He was slow when everything in him wanted to drop both of their bottoms and thrust into her.

Any other woman he was with, he wouldn't think twice.

They'd know what they were getting with him.

Not his time.

Not his attention.

They'd want his wealth and his body and he'd give them enough to make sure they stayed around for his needs then he'd push them along when he had his fill.

Abby had been different from day one.

She didn't know who he was.

Though she might be able to find out easily enough. He was pretty sure she hadn't done an internet search. She'd find him if she did.

Instead, she had dinner with him last night. They swam

with some fish today, ate sandwiches on a boat and then she lay out in the sun while he was trying to close a business deal that was giving him fits.

He should still be on the phone negotiating, but he saw her sitting here in the sun and said that only a stupid man would ignore her.

No one could ever say he wasn't smart.

Their kiss just continued with no tongue action until she pushed her way in.

It was better to let her make that move.

What he didn't expect was how aggressive she'd get with it.

Their mouths were angling left and right, her body was clinging to his and her tongue was thrusting in and out.

Then she found herself underwater and he pulled her up quickly.

"My legs stopped moving," she said, laughing.

"Guess I didn't do that good of a job keeping you afloat."

"I'd like to think you had other things on your mind."

"Definitely that," he said.

He started to move them closer to the shore so her feet were on the sand.

"Can I say I like that you are being so considerate and gentlemanly?"

He wasn't sure any woman had said that to him. His mother would be proud. Much prouder than if she knew the type of women he was normally with and what he did with them.

"No reason to rush," he said. "Vacation is about relaxing."

"It is," she said. "I just don't do these things."

Which he figured as much. "You don't have to do anything you don't want to."

"See. There is that too."

She turned and walked out of the water, her ass beckoning him to follow. He did, like a man in a trance. She climbed the few steps on the dock, got her towel and put it around her.

He found himself mirroring her moves without thought. As if she'd cast a spell on him that he'd never seen coming.

"Want to explain that?"

She sighed. "It's pretty obvious we've lived different lives," she said. "I've lived in the same town my whole life. I even commuted to college and lived at home. It was cheaper and I have loans. I didn't want to leave my father either."

"Was there a reason you didn't want to leave your father?"

"Not bad," she said. "Just that he did so much for me and Liz and he was helping out with school and my car. Lots of things. He took care of us and I wanted to take care of him. I tried to cook and clean and do those things for him. In the summer he's just not around much. The winter is different. I didn't want him to be alone."

He found that commendable. "I was the same way with my mother," he admitted.

"You had to be with that many siblings and your mother being alone. Like my sister Liz, I bet you had to grow up faster than you should have."

There were very few people in the world who would have any sympathy for him. "We do what we need to in life."

"Liz says that too. I never wanted to be a burden to anyone. I think my father was so burdened by my mother. He loved her so much and still blames himself for not being able to help her."

"You can't help someone that doesn't want to be helped," he said.

It felt as if he was preaching to the choir there.

How long had he gone not putting himself first?

It wasn't the same as Abby's father, but on a tiny scale could be.

Maybe deep down he felt there was no help for him. That he'd never find the person who would look at him as West Carlisle the man and not the billionaire.

Having those thoughts in his head made him not even give a woman a chance half the time.

"No," she said. "You can't. Liz told me that for so long. I even feel it at work too."

"How's that?"

"Not that the people I work with are anything compared to what you do. But most of them look at their jobs as that. A job. Not a career. They need money to live and they are working to get what they can to pay the next bill. If people aren't willing to better themselves then they shouldn't complain about the situation they are in."

"There is a ceiling to how much people can better themselves," he said.

"I don't believe that at all," she said.

Her head was angled. "Why?"

"Because if you want something enough, you work at it. Skill, risks and timing are needed. Drive for sure. I mean, I'm not meant to be a CEO by any means. I'm not sure I'd want to be the HR Director because I don't like people being mad at me."

"Someone is always going to be mad at you," he said, smirking.

"True. But my point is, if I wanted it bad enough, I'd go back to school. I'd strive to get there. If I couldn't get there in this company, I'd try another one. I'd move for better opportunities. There shouldn't be a ceiling if I'm willing to do those things. I'm not though."

She made a good point.

He was a prime example of everything she said, but he couldn't very well tell her that.

That he was working class poor more than middle class due to the number in the household. Lots of mouths to feed and his mother didn't work. Daycare would be too expensive. She only got a job when Talia was in school full time and even then it was one with flexible hours to allow for her transporting kids around when needed.

The fact his personal life suffered to put his family and the need to take care of them first couldn't have happened if there was a ceiling.

He went to college.

He got his MBA.

He worked the entire time he was in school and took advantage of every opportunity he could.

He was driven... as Abby said.

Every loan he could get for his father being a member of the military, he did.

He found investors and took risks when others wouldn't or couldn't.

He got to where he was because *nothing* was going to stop him.

Not even the need to have a woman he could come home to every night and tell his day to.

Those early years, no one put up with him not being around.

His determination to succeed in everything but his home life was all he cared about.

No woman wanted to be put second. He was lucky if he was putting someone third or fourth.

"You're right," he said. "Most people just don't want things bad enough."

"Nothing wrong with that," she said. "We all have to do what is right for us. I'm happy in my job."

"Didn't sound it to me."

He'd heard her talking to her sister when he shouldn't have been eavesdropping.

"I get taken advantage of at work," she said, sighing. "I'm the nice one. I've learned the art of being diplomatic to get what I need, but it takes a lot of work when others just put their foot down in the beginning. Or talk around people, lying and manipulating. I can't be that way."

"We all have a way of communicating to get us what we want or need."

"You're direct and to the point. I can be with a side of sunshine. People don't tend to take that seriously though."

"I am," he said.

"Because you don't know me that well and we are on vacation. How did we get talking about this?"

"You're the one that wanted to talk," he pointed out. "You said dinner in if we talked."

"I did say that," she said, giggling. "And it seems I'm doing all the talking. I don't normally open up that much. Tell me something interesting about you."

"The fact that I'm the oldest of eight kids isn't interesting?" he asked. "Most people think that."

"What are their names?" she said. "Or don't you want me to know that?"

"No reason not to. In order. Me, Braylon, Laken, Foster, Elias, Rowan, Nelson, and Talia."

"Wow," she said. "Interesting names."

"My mother likes to be different. None of the names are 'made up' but they aren't common either."

"Some are surnames," she said.

"Yes," he admitted. "I've got my mother's maiden name."

Abby would just assume it was West and not Westerly. It didn't make a difference in his eyes.

"Do any of the rest of the surnames have a meaning?" she asked.

He'd never told anyone this before. "Foster and Nelson. They were two men who were close to my father at different points in his career. They lost their lives. It was their surnames."

"Loyalty," she said. "I find you don't see a lot of it in people much anymore."

"No," he said. "Unless it's family."

Which just made him feel like shit once again for the way he'd been with his own family in the past few years.

The way he was absent when maybe they needed more than money or an opportunity from him.

"That's right," she said. "Family, that's what there is. At least for me. I know a lot of people who aren't close to their family and I feel bad for them. What are your parents' names?"

"My father was Sam, my mother is Aileen."

"Normal names," she said, laughing. "My father is Trevor and my mother is Lily. You know Liz is my sister. Her fiancé is Christian."

"Why don't we go in and figure out what to order for dinner and then we can talk some more?"

"What do you want to talk about?" she asked.

He normally spent most of his time talking about work. Boring things to Abby he was sure.

The last thing he wanted to do was think about work, and for a man who lived his life making the next dollar to take care of his family, he was at a loss.

"Why don't we pull topics out of a bag?"

"Seriously?" she asked.

"Sure," he said. "It can be fun, right?"

"I think that's great. We can ask silly questions like our first car or favorite food or activity and then talk more about it if we want."

He wasn't sure he'd ever told anyone those things or that a woman would care enough.

"Anything you want," he said.

She leaned in and gave him a big smacking kiss on the lips. "Thank you."

"What for?" he asked.

"Just not laughing at me. I guess sometimes you get to know someone better when you do fun things like that. No one is guarded or thinking there is some ulterior motive. I don't have one. Never did and don't think I ever will."

She was too genuine in her reactions, responses and her words for him to believe she might be lying. He hated to think she was naive, but he was betting she was by a lot of people's standards.

"You're such a breath of fresh air," he said.

"Not sure anyone has ever said that before, but I'll take it. I mean you live in Manhattan, I've got to imagine the air isn't all that fresh."

He threw his head back and laughed. "You have no idea."

8

THAT FINAL STEP

"I can't believe I'm leaving tomorrow," Abby said.

The time had just flown by.

She'd spent all day Tuesday with West. Wednesday he picked her up for lunch and they drove around and did some shopping while she grabbed a few things for her sister and father.

Today, he'd gotten her again for lunch and they were going to take a three-hour cruise around the island. That was his idea and she was all for it.

"You need to be at the airport at eleven," he said.

"I do. My flight leaves around one, but I need to check out by ten anyway, so I'll do that and get a taxi and just spend the time in the airport."

"I'll bring you," he said.

"No," she said. "You said you've got things to do."

She knew he was leaving tomorrow too but hadn't said when he was. That he had a few things to do on the island. She didn't ask what either. It wasn't her business. They didn't waste their time talking about work even though she knew he was doing that in the mornings before they met up.

"It's fine," he said. "It's on the way. Don't worry."

"Well, we do have to check out at the same time."

"That's right," he said. "So don't worry about it."

"If you say so," she said. He parked his car in the parking lot and they walked to the boat they'd be on for the lunch cruise.

When they were settled into seats, he said, "This is a private cruise."

"What?" she asked. "This is a huge boat. I thought we were waiting for other people."

"Nope," he said. "Just for us. Only waiting for one more staff. I think they are bringing some special food."

"Special food?" she asked. "Are you getting a burger?"

He'd been eating fish and trying not to complain about the fact that he couldn't get a steak. She found it funny.

"Maybe," he said, grinning adorably.

"I don't even want to know how you managed that."

Or how much this whole day had cost.

Not once had he let her pay for anything and it was frustrating.

Nope, that was wrong. Yesterday while they were walking around the shops she bought them a frozen dessert. She didn't know the name of what they had, only that it was delicious and she ate it as fast as she could. West doing the same.

He thanked her and kissed her on the street, putting his arm around her.

Kissing was all that they'd done and not once had he asked for anything more.

No pressure. No hints other than his hands moving around but keeping them PG just the same.

The fact he was doing that and it was her last full day

and she didn't think she'd ever see him again, was all the more reason to take that final step.

Yes, she had his number. They'd been communicating the whole time here when they weren't together, but she was sure once they were back in New York, reality would step in and she'd be the poor girl he spent a few nice days with in his eyes.

He'd be that once-in-a-lifetime thing that came with this trip that she could hold onto for memories to come for the rest of her life.

She'd learned to not ask for more and never hope for it.

Life just didn't work that way for her. She was fine with it too.

She didn't think she'd be equipped for more with him being so far away when they returned home.

"Anything is possible if you ask nice enough," he said, laughing.

Abby didn't believe it.

She knew he had money but let it go. It intimidated her, but it wasn't anything she'd worry about after here.

Everything they did was his suggestion other than the snorkeling. She was fine with it though. He'd asked her if she had things she wanted to do and she didn't come up with much.

Maybe because she knew he wouldn't let her pay for it.

"We are ready to take off," one of the crew said.

West put his arm around her shoulder and pulled her close as the boat went into reverse and they pulled away.

"This has been the best few days of my life," she said. "Thank you so much. I mean even if I didn't meet you it would have been great, but meeting you has just put the cherry on the sundae."

"Thanks," he said. "I have to say I would have never enjoyed my time here nearly as much without you."

She poked him in the side with her finger. "I think you would have worked the whole time."

"I would have," he said. "So my employees thank you and don't even know it."

She let it slide that he said his employees. She was positive he had people working for him. He had to with the amount of work he'd been doing on his vacation and the number of calls or texts he'd try to not take around her.

An hour went by while they set sail and one of the crew brought out a tray with silver domes on it.

"Lunch is served," she said. "Can't wait to see what it is."

There were four domes.

"Not sure what you wanted. You seem to like fish."

"I can eat just about anything. I do like fish but never cook it myself so this is a treat."

Each cover was taken off. There were two massive burgers with fries and she started to laugh.

"I had two made in case you wanted one too."

"That was nice of you," she said.

The other two showed a salad with a beautifully cooked salmon and the third some lobster dish.

"What are you thinking?" he asked. "Or do you want some of everything?"

Her eyes looked him over, from the top of his brown hair to the beard that had gotten a little thicker and he'd often scratch it, over his gray T-shirt, navy shorts, down to his bare feet.

"I think I want just about everything I see today," she said.

His smile just lit up his face as if it were the moon over the water at night. "Then you should get what you want."

Hours later, they were back at his place. They rarely stayed at hers and she didn't care. They were identical in size and what was offered.

They'd had a huge late lunch and she didn't think she'd have room to eat anything other than a piece of fruit for hours.

What she had in mind was to burn it off by getting West naked.

The looks he'd been sending her all afternoon said he was more than willing.

She found it funny he wasn't making the move though.

"So," she said. "Are you going to make me do it?"

"Do what?" he asked. He had the doors open to the ocean view allowing them to move from the small living space to the covered area outside.

"Make a move," she said.

"Come here," he said, holding his hand out.

She walked closer and he yanked her hard into his chest, forcing her to let out a laugh.

"That was nice."

"You're calling the shots," he said. "I remember the woman from the first night getting pressure from a stranger. Though I don't think we are strangers, it's only been a few days. If you want to sit and watch the sunset like we've been doing and then have me walk you back to your place, I will. If you want to stay and talk, we can do that. If you tell me to strip you naked and take you on my bed with the view in the distance, I'll gladly do that."

"The last option, please," she said, smiling.

"Thank God," he said, picking her up and carrying her into his room.

He set her on her feet and then moved to open the glass

doors to let the breeze and magic of the island into the room with them.

When she would have pulled her shirt over her head, he stopped her.

"Do you want to take it off?" she asked

"I do," he said. "I said strip you and that is what I'm going to do."

"Do I get to do the same to you?"

"Absolutely," he said.

"And I should ask if you've got a condom since I don't. It's not like I came on this trip planning this."

"I do," he said.

He put his hands on her cheeks, his mouth lowered to hers, and this kiss was anything but soft and slow.

This was an experienced man who was going to show her what she'd been missing her entire life.

She was going to give herself over to him too.

He didn't stop kissing her to lift her shirt over her head until it was yanked off, then his mouth returned, his hands quickly unclasping her bra and gliding over her skin. She wasn't sure how it happened, but he was cupping her breasts as the angle of the kiss changed once again.

Their tongues were dueling and she moaned when he applied some pressure to her puckered nipple.

When his mouth left hers she wanted to protest but couldn't when he put it on the nipple that felt neglected.

It sure didn't when his tongue was darting around.

Her knees went weak and she thought she was going down to the ground, but he caught her, had her in his arms and moved her to the bed to lay her down.

"I think I've got to just treasure you for a few hours."

"Hours?" she squeaked out. "I'm not sure I can last five minutes."

He laughed. That deep one that vibrated in his chest and almost sent sonic waves to her wet heat making her want to lean up and grind against him.

"Nothing says we can't do this a few times if you're up for it."

"I can be if you are," she said. "I know you're older than me."

"Not funny," he said, laughing.

"Nope," she said. "I'm not laughing. I'm just hoping you took your vitamins so you can keep the promise you're throwing out there."

He scooted down and pulled her shorts off with her panties. "I've been wondering about this."

She was shaved bare. She always was. It was just easier and part of her daily routine when she shaved her legs.

"No need to wonder anymore," she said.

He didn't reply.

Just dipped his head and licked the length of her.

She squealed.

"You like that," he said.

"I think I'd like any touch there. You haven't done anything special yet."

"Now you're just trying to make me work harder," he said. "I like it."

She hadn't meant to even say those words and didn't know where they came from but at least was happy he didn't get annoyed over them.

It was the last thought she had though other than the feelings being assaulted in her body.

West had her legs spread wide, his arms under her thighs and lifted and he went all in as if it were a feast he hadn't had in years.

He was licking her.

He was sucking on her.

He was bringing her to the edge so many times and then leaving her hanging there.

Wanting.

Needing.

Begging.

He finally gave in and latched onto her bud and didn't let go.

She screamed out his name, bucked up harder into his face and couldn't stop until she was so exhausted it felt as if she ran miles in the burning sun to get this.

"That was so worth it," she said, sighing.

He laughed, then moved up and kissed her on the mouth.

"Now that you're relaxed, how about letting me get a little fantasy out of my head?"

She hadn't known her eyes were shut but opened them. "Depends what it is."

"Nothing that far out there," he said. "The first time I got my hands on you, you were in the lounge chair looking out at the ocean. I was rubbing your back, your legs, I was thinking of taking you just like that as we both took in the view."

The words had more heat flooding through her body, making her wonder if she was dripping on the sheets.

She couldn't answer, just nodded her head.

He stood up and started to undress while she watched him.

She knew he had a great chest on him. Toned legs, and nice biceps.

Now she saw he had one hell of a member to go with the rest of his body.

"Wow," she said.

"Thanks," he said. "I think."

There was humor in his voice and she didn't care.

He got the condom out, covered himself, and she turned to lie on her stomach at the foot of the bed, facing out at the view beyond.

His hands went to her back and started to rub and massage. She hadn't realized it, but he had lotion on them again.

The cool silky feeling glided over her shoulders and arms, down her back.

No clothing to dip his fingers under so he just covered her arms and kept going.

A little more lotion had him doing it to her legs and the light smell of vanilla was almost as intoxicating as what he was doing to her.

"West. You know how to torture someone. I was thinking the same thing but wouldn't have said that to you days ago."

"I know you were," he said.

There was the cocky man she knew was inside and that he hadn't shown much.

It seemed to her it came out in tiny doses as if it was second nature rather than something he had to show off.

She liked it better that way. A confidence that was part of who he was and not someone who had to make people believe something that wasn't true.

His chest touched her back, the weight of his body a comfort she'd never felt before.

Her legs spread as his hands slid over her arms, found her fingers and entwined them together.

Everything he did, every move he made, had a purpose.

To give her the most pleasure possible at the same time in multiple locations.

He'd entered her the moment their fingers twisted

together and she felt her body sigh in satisfaction.

His hips were moving forward and back.

Nothing hard.

Nothing fast.

Just slow and steady and letting her know that was what a man did when he treasured a woman.

His lips found her neck, started to kiss her and moved up to her earlobes. "You okay?" he asked.

She hummed in her throat, not sure she could say much more.

But a minute later, she had to speak. "I can't believe how close I am again."

She was panting now. "Good," he said.

He continued a steady movement as if he had all the time in the world. How the hell was this possible? Did he not feel as strongly as her?

"I'm going to come again," she said and then everything just exploded like the finale of the July Fourth fireworks show.

As her body was throbbing, it was as if that was the sign he needed to let go.

He was moving faster now, his hands gripping her tightly, his breath in her ear hard and harsh.

The bed was squeaking like a bunch of exotic birds chirping outside, but all she knew was that *she* was bringing this out of him.

Then he just stopped and dropped on her.

She felt him coming inside of her and there was a bucket full of pride over what the two of them just experienced.

Too bad today was the last day she'd ever feel this way again.

But tomorrow was a day away. This was now and this was for them.

9

ABOUT THE FUTURE

"You're going to text me when you land," West said on Friday morning. "Right?"

Abby laughed at him. He'd packed up and loaded his stuff into the rental car, then went to help Abby with her things.

"You'll be in the air too," she said.

"So?" he said. "I want to know that you landed."

He didn't want this day to end. He wasn't sure the last time he felt like this in his life. If ever.

The fact he put so much work off to spend it with a woman he'd just met wasn't like him.

She asked nothing of him. She wanted to do things *for* him.

No way he'd take it.

He didn't even want her to buy him their fruity ice the other day, but he said that was being stupid. She had her pride too and jokingly told him that.

"Then I'll text," she said.

He knew he would have left days ago if he hadn't met her. He would have loved nothing more than to stay a few extra days. He could have. He had his place until Sunday but didn't tell her that.

Instead he called Vanessa and told her to set his jet up to come get him on Friday.

She'd laughed and said he'd lasted longer than anyone thought. They even had a pool going in the office.

He wasn't surprised to hear that. He didn't bother to ask who won.

"Make sure you do," he said, grabbing her bag for her and walking out to the car to put it in the trunk.

"You didn't need to bring me," she said.

"Maybe I'm not ready to let you go," he said.

"Back to reality," she said. "I know. It's been fun."

That sounded like she was saying goodbye.

Nope.

No one did that until he was ready.

He was by no means ready to end what this could be.

"Don't say that," he said. "I'm a few hours away. This could be easy."

She laughed. "West. We are two different people with completely opposite lives."

"What does that mean?"

No way she knew who he was. He was positive of it. He'd tackle that when they returned. She'd find out soon enough, he was sure.

The fact she didn't look into him on this trip was everything he needed to know about her and what she valued in life.

"It means you live this fancy classy life in a big city. I rent a tiny apartment and ended up on a vacation of a lifetime by winning it. I'm going back to my job which pays the bills and gives me some tiny savings. We don't live in each other's world."

That thought never occurred to him.

"I didn't think you were afraid of things."

"Don't play that game," she said, laughing. "I'm not falling for it."

"It was worth a shot," he said, shrugging with a smirk. He started the car once they were buckled in and then drove to the airport. His hand went to hers. "I'm being serious. At the core of it, we aren't that much different. We have very similar backgrounds and upbringings. You know that."

They didn't talk about their personal lives much and he was fine with it.

Instead they found out more of the fun things. The stuff they did in college. Favorite holidays. Time with their siblings.

He guessed he needed that too.

To think of what it was like when he wasn't the fill-in father and was rather the big brother beating on his brothers.

Dodging things Laken threw at him for picking on her.

The boys he intimidated when they wanted to talk to his sister.

Yeah, the normal things he'd forgotten existed in his life.

The man his sister said he used to be had come back some this week. He realized he had missed it more than he could have imagined and wanted it to continue.

He knew he'd need Abby for that though.

"We do have some similar things. We didn't talk about tomorrow. Not even tonight. I just want you to know I don't have any expectations."

"So noted," he said. "Why can't we give this a try? People do all the time."

"We can," she said. "If you want to. But if you get back to your life and are too busy to come see me, or have me drive there, I understand too. I've never thought I could be someone to do a long-distance relationship."

He wouldn't accept that. "I won't be too busy," he said.

"You say that now because you're thinking of the fact I could barely get out of bed and walk to the bathroom to shower this morning."

They'd made love so many times he'd lost count. Then in the shower did it again.

She laughed and said she was waving the white flag.

He couldn't get enough of her.

The fear that she was going to walk out of his life was like nothing he thought he'd ever feel with a woman.

"There is that too," he said, laughing.

"Let's just talk about the fun things we did this week," she said. "Not about the future."

He thought he heard her voice catch and decided to honor that.

It wasn't as long as he'd hoped when they got to the airport. He pulled into the drop-off lane, got her bag out and hugged her tight enough to last her the trip home.

Or maybe it was to last him the trip home. Then they kissed like his mother used to do to his father before he left for months at a time.

That thought only depressed him when it popped into his head and he wondered where that suppressed memory came from.

It was as if meeting Abby was bringing out all the things he'd locked up in his life.

Like his grief.

Yep, not going there.

He'd built his reputation of taking no mercy in his life and wasn't going to show any weakness.

"Text me," he said again.

"I will," she said. "I promise."

West gave her one more kiss, then watched her walk away, heard a horn beeping and ignored it.

Once she was out of sight, he went back to the car to return his rental. She didn't need to know he'd be going to another terminal and getting on his jet.

He'd be home before her. He was leaving first and it was a nonstop flight.

He'd wanted to bring her with him. He could have made sure they landed in Albany.

It wasn't the time to let her know though.

A struggle he had on the last day.

But he'd told himself that leaving on good terms rather than having her mad at him on the flight back, which was a massive possibility, was better.

When he was on his jet forty minutes later waiting for takeoff, he pulled his laptop out to get some work done.

He had to distract himself from Abby and knowing they were going to be separated.

When his phone vibrated he picked it up to see the text from her saying she had the best time ever and thanked him for everything.

She'd thanked him so many times that it was getting annoying, but he wouldn't show it.

He was just glad she reached out first.

He typed back to stop thanking him and that he had just as much of a great time as her.

She sent him a heart back. The first she'd done something like that.

He didn't want to read more into it and wouldn't send one back.

But he did pull up a bunch of the pictures he'd taken of

her on the trip and started to scroll through them with a smile on his face.

"Looks as if you had a great trip," Susie said.

His flight attendant that he paid dearly to be available when he needed her. Susie was in her forties, married and had a few kids. She treated him like a younger brother. Something he'd never experienced before. He liked it.

"I did," he said, putting his phone away.

"The tan looks good on you," Susie said. "Maybe you should get outside more often."

"I've been hearing that a lot lately," he said. "I think I'll start to listen more."

"Good," Susie said. "We are getting ready to take off. Can I get you your normal drink?"

"How about a club soda," he said. "Let's try something a little different."

"Looks as if you've been trying a lot different," Susie said, winking.

He wondered if she'd seen the pictures he was looking at but knew she wouldn't say a word either.

10

RISKY BUSINESS

"It sounds as if you had the best time imaginable," Liz said to her Saturday morning at her apartment.

"Everything but the flight home," Abby said.

Talk about a horrible way to end her trip. At her layover in Georgia, there was a problem with the plane and she was stuck there for eight hours, getting into Albany close to midnight.

No way she was texting West that happened, so she'd told him she was stuck and what the plan was. She'd reach out today.

She was still on the fence doing it, but would. Maybe.

It'd taken him thirty minutes to return her text that he was sorry she was stuck.

She wasn't sure why he was sorry. It's not like it was anything he'd done.

"That stinks," Liz said. "Traveling is always risky business."

"It is," she said. "So by the time I got home, I took a shower, had a snack and then climbed into bed. I got up an hour ago, showered and ate and was going to do my laundry."

"Guess I shouldn't have come over so early," Liz said.

"No, I'm glad you did. I need to talk to you."

She had to tell someone about West. More so when she saw the little gift he'd left in her bag.

She'd been stunned and wasn't sure how he did it.

"What's going on?" Liz asked. "Can I get you a coffee or something?"

"Coffee works," Abby said. "It will go well with the donuts. Not that I need any other sugar or calories. I ate so much while I was there."

Liz had showed up with jelly donuts. One of the things she'd loved as a kid. She could always count on her big sister to be there for her.

"You could use a few pounds," Liz said.

"Says no woman ever," she said, laughing. "But it's not like I sat still all that much. I felt as if I walked so much I burned it off."

"I can't wait to see more pictures. The ones you sent me were awesome. Christian is all on board to go there."

"You'll love it," she said. She took a deep breath. "I met someone."

"Huh?" Liz asked, biting into the sugary donut.

There was a time her sister wouldn't eat anything like that. Liz's ex-husband had controlled and verbally abused her. Told her she was fat when she was anything but.

Abby was glad to know her sister didn't hold any negative feelings about eating or enjoying life as a result.

It was partially because of Christian and the other part because her sister had always been so strong.

"His name is West Carlisle. He was at the resort with

me." She went on to tell her sister how West saved her from the guy hitting on her.

"I'm glad I didn't know about this the night it happened," Liz said.

"Trust me, I get it. I was very careful. It's just he was so nice and sweet and he said he did it because I reminded him of his sister. He had given me so many opportunities to trust him."

"You trust no one," Liz said.

"Not true. I trust you and Dad."

"Sorry," Liz said. "You don't trust men in general."

"I know. I don't. I don't even know if I trust him other than I told myself it was a short-term thing."

"You had a fling," Liz said, pointing her finger. "Did you sleep with him?"

"I did. On Thursday night. I waited and he never once pressured me."

"That's a nice feeling, isn't it?" Liz asked. "Is that it now? You're never going to see him again?"

"He lives in Manhattan. He wanted me to text him when I got home. I told him what happened with the flight, but I wasn't going to text him at midnight when I landed." Though she was positive he was probably up working.

"I wouldn't have either. Are you going to today?"

"I think so," she said. "I've got to show you something." She moved to the counter where the jewelry box was. "These were in my bag with a note."

Her sister read the note that said what a wonderful time he'd had, then she flipped the lid to show the diamond hoop earrings.

"Whoa," Liz said. "That's some bling."

"I doubt they are real."

"If they are it's a massive gift to give someone you just met."

"That's right," she said. "I mean he had a rented Mercedes. He was staying in a really expensive place. He had class and all. But come on. People don't do that."

"What does he do for a living?" Liz asked.

"I never really asked for details. I just assumed he was some boss or something in an office. The way he scratched his beard told me he was trying to be someone he wasn't."

"Which would have bothered you but yet you spent time with him. Why?"

"I don't know. Maybe I thought it'd be fun. Or that he just didn't want to shave. It was nothing more than that. He seemed like someone who worked a ton and told me a few times I gave him a break from it."

"Just like you needed a break too. Did you do a search on him?"

"No," she said. "It felt rude. I mean I wouldn't want someone to do it on me. I'm going to bet he's not on any type of common social media. He's not the type to be on Facebook."

Liz laughed. "I'm going to look him up now."

"You don't think it's rude?" she asked.

"Abby! You slept with the guy. He gave you earrings worth thousands of dollars."

"No way," she said. "They've got to be fake. Why would someone do that?"

"I don't know," Liz said. "Which is why it makes sense to look into him." Her sister's jaw dropped while she was on her phone. "Oh my. Is this him?"

Abby pulled the phone out of her sister's hand and read the headline, "Billionaire West Carlisle in talks to buy a majority share of the New York Hawks."

She had no idea he liked hockey. It never came up once.

Then she shook her head and looked closer at the man in the picture, zooming in on her sister's phone.

"He's clean shaven there and in a fancy suit. I mean I think it's him. No, it can't be."

This was crazy. You didn't just meet some billionaire on an island and have sex with him.

"Hang on," Liz said, scrolling around. "Here is another picture with what looks like three other people with the same last name as him. Maybe siblings, but they are employees too."

"He told me his siblings' names," she said. "Braylon."

"Who is an attorney," Liz said.

"Shit," she said. "The others are Laken, Foster, Elias, Rowan, Nelson, Talia. There are eight of them. He's the oldest."

"Looks like four of them in this picture."

She grabbed the phone again and looked. There was West. He had a day growth of beard, was in jeans and a button-down shirt looking more normal to her. Next to him was his brother Elias, sister Laken and brother Braylon. It was an article about a brewery he'd just purchased and his brother was running in North Carolina.

"Oh my God," she said. "He lied to me."

"Did he?" Liz asked, laughing.

"What? How can you say that?'

"You know his siblings. You just said their names. You know the one was an attorney."

"I know what they all do for the most part. It just doesn't make sense. His father died in the service when West was eighteen. He pretty much helped raise the rest of them. Did he lie to me about his parents?"

She was scrolling through any article she could find and then typed in West's name and parents and found an article.

Liz took her phone back. "Looks like you've got your answers. His name is Westerly. Did you know that?"

"No. I joked about his name and his siblings' names being different or surnames. He said he was named after his mother's maiden name."

"Looks like his mother is Aileen Westerly-Carlisle. Still not a lie."

"Still not a lie," she agreed. She sat down. This was too much to process. "What am I going to do?"

"Maybe text him," Liz said.

"Come on now," she said. "He's a billionaire. These earrings have to be real. I've never owned anything like this. What would he want to do with me? I don't even think I have the value of these earrings in my savings account. Not to mention I don't do long-distance anything. I can't see how any of this would work even if he did have the money to help it along."

"Maybe you reminded him of where he came from," Liz said.

"That doesn't make me feel better," she said sadly. Talk about knocking her down.

"It's not meant to make you feel bad. I'm just saying it seems as if he had some humble beginnings. Not so different than us."

"But why would he want to go back? I've got nothing to offer him."

"Don't sell yourself short," Liz said firmly. "You don't know anything until you talk to him."

"I feel like this was all a joke to him," she said. She

started to sniffle some. "I live here. He lives there. I don't or can't live anywhere like that. I'd feel like a fish out of water in Manhattan to visit let alone being around him."

If she'd known he was a billionaire beforehand, she wouldn't have been as open with him.

She'd fear he was judging her and she'd been judged enough in her life.

She hoped he wasn't laughing at her behind her back.

There was no way she wanted to reach out to him now.

"You don't know until you talk to him. You know, like Cinderella."

"That's a fairytale and it doesn't happen to people like us."

"A year ago I'd agree with you. But every day I see Christian and know I got my fairytale come true. Not that Christian is a billionaire, but he's not doing half bad."

Her sister was laughing at her.

This was the sister she had when she was growing up. Not the one who left home and spent years in a horrible marriage.

"He's great. But we are talking about me," she said.

"That's right. I think you should text him and give him shit about who he is."

"I can't do that," she argued.

"That's your problem. You can but you won't. You don't want anyone mad at you. Here is the thing. If you don't think anything can come of this, then why does it matter if you tell him that you don't like feeling as if you were played? If you think something might come of it, then be honest now or it's only going to fester anyway."

"Nothing at all can come about from this," she said.

"That's up to you to find out," Liz said. "But you can't

find out anything if you don't reach out. Unless you think he'll reach out to you?"

"I need a few days to think about this," she said. "It's not like I'm going anywhere or run the risk of running into him."

11

_____

GREAT THINGS HAPPEN

"Earth to West," Braylon said to him on Monday morning. "Your body is here, but is your brain still in Aruba?"

"What?" he asked his brother.

"I said you haven't been yourself since I walked into your office. You're always preoccupied but can still do ten things at once. You're scattered right now. What is going on?"

Braylon knew him the best.

They were the closest.

His brother and he went through all the growing pains earlier on together.

Braylon could have started his own firm. He could have gone to work anywhere when he graduated.

He stuck it out with West knowing the two of them were going to make great things happen.

No, Braylon wasn't the top dog in the legal department, but his brother would get there.

"Just a lot on my mind. You know I'm dealing with the Hawks' purchase."

"I don't understand why you want to own more of it," Braylon said. "You don't even go to any games."

"Dad loved hockey," he said absently.

"Yeah," Braylon said. "He did. But you don't."

"It's a good investment and the price is right," he argued.

"Fine. But you've had multiple deals going on most of your life and yet you are all over the place now," Braylon said.

There was a knock at the door and his sister walked in.

"Look at you. You've got a tan. I bet you've got a mark on your legs from where your laptop was the whole time."

"Very funny," he said.

His mother gave him grief for not being there for his siblings, but it didn't stop them from busting his ass.

He supposed he should be thankful he didn't mess up too much lately with them.

Didn't mean his other siblings weren't ticked off, but Talia was happy with the necklace he'd sent to her.

"Seriously, it does look like you relaxed some. And you must have been taking some time away. There were gaps when I didn't get an email or text," Braylon said.

"So it wasn't just me he wasn't bugging?" Laken asked. "Our big brother might have actually gone on vacation and...relaxed?"

"I did," he said. "And now I'm back and playing catch-up more than normal so don't give me shit if I'm distracted."

No reason to say the distraction came in the form of a blonde-haired beauty that he'd worried about as she was stuck in Georgia at the airport.

He was kicking himself for not offering her the flight home with him. Then he wanted to send his jet to get her home.

Nope, he didn't do any of it and waited for that text to tell him she got home safely.

It didn't come on Saturday. Not Sunday either.

He wondered what was going through her head.

Did she find out who he was?

He was pretty sure that was the case.

Was she waiting for him to make the move?

He was going to have to. He knew it.

But he wanted Abby to do it first on Saturday and it didn't happen.

He tried to convince himself that she was busy doing things.

Then Sunday came and went and nothing.

Today she'd be back to work and catching up after a week off.

How long was he going to keep making excuses?

He wasn't ready to walk away. He just couldn't.

He was going to have to make that move and would do it tonight.

"I won't take up too much of your time," Laken said. "I'm surprised you wanted to meet today."

"I told you I was going to try to meet weekly with you," he said. "Both of you. That is what today is about."

"Mom really got to you, didn't she?" Braylon asked, smirking.

"It's not about Mom."

"I heard she and Talia got you so good," Laken said.

"Did Talia tell you?"

"Of course. We two girls have to stick together."

His sisters were eleven years apart. They didn't have a lot in common for most of their lives.

Even now Laken would complain that Talia was so different than her.

But as Abby had said, family was always there.

"It's over now," he said. "Let's get to work."

"How come you didn't make Foster come in?" he asked.

"Foster never comes into the city," Braylon said. "If West wants to meet with him in person he's going to have to go to see him."

"Foster already laid the law down. Video calls or I'm going to him," he said.

Most would think it was odd that as the CEO of his own billion-dollar empire, he wasn't telling his brother to just get his ass here.

But he wasn't like that. Or tried not to be despite all of them bitching about him to his mother.

He knew his siblings' strengths and weaknesses and how they thrived.

There was no reason to push his brother to come here when it wasn't needed. Not when he knew the day might come when it would be needed.

"Let's get to work," Braylon said. "I've got a shit ton of meetings this afternoon."

"I'm catching a flight out of here in a few hours," Laken said.

"Where are you going?" West asked.

Laken's face almost mirrored Braylon's in shock. "You told Laken you needed her in Colorado to deal with your newest acquisition."

"Yeah," he said. "You need to be there."

He was investing in a shoe line using recycled materials. Laken was going to go in and give them the lay of the land on what it was like to be part of his enterprise. To more or less orientate them to the way things were done.

They'd been waiting for the last of the deal to go

through and last week it was finalized. One of those things he had to handle while he was in Aruba.

"That is where I'm going," Laken said. "I'll be back Thursday at the latest."

He nodded and the three of them got down to more business. "If you both need to meet with me separately this week, let me know."

"I'm good," Braylon said. "I can come down and get you if I need you."

Braylon was good like that. Not like he did it often though. Texts were more their way of communication.

"I'm fine," Laken said. "We can plan on something next week."

"I'll have Vanessa schedule you in," he said and then got to work when they left.

But work wasn't coming when three rolled around and he felt as if he hadn't accomplished much.

He couldn't get his mind off of Abby or stop wondering if she was thinking of him.

Missing him.

Pissed at him.

Yeah, he was thinking it was the last one.

He picked his phone up and rather than send her a text, called.

It rang four times and he thought for sure it'd go to voicemail, but it didn't.

"Hello, Westerly? Or do you prefer just West?"

Yep. She figured it out.

"West," he said. "I would have told you my name was Westerly if that is what I went by. It's not like you introduced yourself as Abigail though I'm sure that is your name."

"You mean you didn't have me looked into?" she asked.

He'd done that in the past, but it didn't occur to him to do that with Abby.

Where the hell was his mind at that he hadn't?

"No," he said. "Is there a reason I need to?"

"I'd think someone of your means would want to know everything about the women they are spending time with."

"You're annoyed with me," he said simply.

"I'm not sure what I am. I think I'm embarrassed more than anything."

He'd rather have annoyance or anger than think she was hurt or upset.

"There is nothing to be embarrassed about," he said. "Why would you say that?"

"I feel like a fool," she said quietly.

Her voice caught and he realized this was a mistake. Calling her and not being able to see her in person.

"Don't."

"I should have just done a search on you when I was in Aruba like a normal person does. Then I would have known."

"And you wouldn't have spent any time with me, right?"

There was silence to that. "I don't know. I mean, I knew you had a big important job, but I didn't expect this. My sister is engaged to a millionaire. I don't think anything of that. But you're on a completely different level."

"I'm just a guy you met on vacation and spent five days with."

She snorted. "Come on, West. You know that isn't true. You probably had your own private jet take you there and back."

There was no reason to lie.

"I did. I wanted to bring you back. I could have done that

easily. When I found out you were stuck in Georgia I wanted to send my jet there to get you."

She laughed and he knew it wasn't a funny sound. "Do you hear yourself? Those things don't happen in my world."

"It's not a big deal," he said. "But if I offered then you would have known and I didn't want our week to end on an angry note."

"Because you knew I'd be upset," she said. "No one likes to feel like a fool."

"You're not a fool," he said. "Those days with you were the best I've had in probably my entire adult life. For a period of time I could walk away from everything and everyone that I have to carry on my shoulders and just focus on you and us. You have no idea what that is like and how it made me feel. How much I appreciated that."

"So I filled a void for you for then," she said. "Now you're back in your world and I'm in mine."

"I'm not sure why they have to be separate," he said.

"Because you don't fit in here and I definitely don't fit in there."

"I grew up in the same world as you," he said firmly. "Maybe I miss it. My mother, she works in a bookstore."

"You told me. I'm sure it's a bookstore you bought her."

No reason to deny it.

"That's not the point. My mother raised eight kids and should be sitting home and doing anything she wants other than working, but she's not. No one in my family gets a free ride. What is in our bank account means nothing."

"It's easy to say that when you've got so much in there." He didn't know what to say. "West, what is it you want? Just tell me that. Be honest with me."

"I haven't lied to you once and I'm not going to. I want what we had in Aruba."

"We aren't in Aruba anymore," she said plainly.

"No. We are back home and I'm not ready to be done with what we've got."

"Oh," she said. "*You're* not ready. Now that sounds more like the guy I read about."

He ground his teeth. "I didn't mean it that way. What do you want, Abby? Take out of the equation what you found out when you returned. I told you before we left I wanted to keep in touch. That I wanted to see where this went. You never once said what you wanted. Maybe you just wanted to find some guy to have fun with. You said you get taken advantage of all the time. That you don't like people mad at you, but you seem to be standing up for yourself right now."

He heard a sniffle and then another.

Shit, she was crying.

What the fuck was he supposed to do now?

"This can't work," she said. "You're not the person I met there."

"I am," he said. "I'm sorry. I'm frustrated. I should have told you, but would you have even believed me?"

When there was more silence, he hoped he was getting through to her. "Probably not."

"And if I showed you articles online about me, you might think I was bragging," he said.

"Most likely," she said.

"Then it feels as if there was no right way to do this without you getting upset. If I could go back in time to do it differently, I would."

"You mean you can't buy a time machine to do it?" she asked sarcastically.

He laughed at her. "If I could, I would. Right now. I'd do anything to not make you upset or mad at me. Just tell me what it is you need me to say."

"Nothing," she said. "I can't see how this is even real. I'm sorry, West. I had a great time. I'll always remember you and what we did together. There is no way this can work."

She hung up on him.

He wasn't sure anyone had ever hung up on him before.

And that was all the more reason for him to not give up.

This was going to be a challenge and he was up for it.

12

TALKED ABOUT THIS

A t six on Wednesday, Abby heard a knock at her door.

Figuring it had to be a neighbor who wanted to know how her trip was, she answered without looking.

"West," she said, her jaw dropping. "What are you doing here?"

He moved in past her. "You don't seem to want to talk on the phone and I'm not ready to end this without seeing you in person."

Again with *him* not being ready to end it.

"I thought we talked about this," she said.

Her eyes were taking in the sight of him.

No expensive suit that she'd seen him in when she did more research on him.

Funny how everything she found never talked about a significant other.

No pictures either.

If he wasn't with a coworker then it was family in every picture of him online.

For someone his age, she found that odd.

"What are you looking at?" he asked her.

"What?"

"You're looking at me. Why? What are you thinking?"

She felt her face flush. "Just because I'm attracted to you doesn't mean we can have anything that works," she admitted.

"It doesn't mean we can't try either," he said, reaching forward and yanking her to his chest.

His mouth crushed hers and she felt as if she was transported back into the heat and sun of their vacation fling.

She wasn't even aware her arms went around his neck until he laughed low in his throat.

She pushed back. "Not fair."

"Totally fair," he said.

"That's a childish response," she said, crossing her arms.

He smirked at her. "So was your statement. Are we going to talk like mature adults now?"

She let out a sigh. "Come in," she said. "Try not to judge. I'm sure your bedroom is bigger than my whole apartment."

"See, there you go again," he said. "Making assumptions. I live in a penthouse in Manhattan. Money doesn't always buy that much space."

"Whatever," she said. "It's still nothing you are used to."

He followed her away from the door and she sat on her little love seat. She only had a chair to go with it. Nothing special and something she'd had for years that she'd bought on sale at an outlet store.

"I lived on military bases with a lot of kids. I never had my own room or anything fancy," he said.

"That was then. This is now."

"You're the only one putting us in slots," he argued.

"How did you find me?" she asked. "Someone on staff most likely looked into me and you got my address, right?"

"No," he said. "Believe it or not, I did it myself."

She snorted. "Why?"

"Because what we've got is between us. Maybe I don't want other people to know right now."

"Because you're embarrassed," she said.

"Do I have to kiss you again to shut you up?" He moved over and sat next to where she'd flopped. "I'd gladly do it. It's all I could think about for days. Getting my mouth and hands on your body."

"Okay. So you found me yourself. Did you take your jet to get here?" she asked.

He sighed. "I've got the means to get here faster. So what?" he said. "It was easier to fly and avoid traffic. Air time was less than an hour."

"And I bet you had a driver take you to the airport and then rented a car here."

"I'd have to rent a car to drive here from the airport. It's a shorter commute from your place to the airport than mine. Convenient for when you come to see me."

"You're doing a lot of assuming," she said. She found it odd he wasn't asking her anything and that the man she spent a week with didn't give orders like he was now.

"I'm good at persuasion," he said smugly.

"You think so," she said, crossing her arms.

"Abby," he said softly. "Do you want me to walk out the door and never come back? Seriously. Be honest. Don't think about all the obstacles. Think about the time we had in Aruba. Think about what it meant for each of us. Then give me your answer."

There was the guy she'd spent time with. Asking nicely. He seemed to be more than one person. "The obstacles are there."

"That isn't an answer."

"Fine," she said. "If they weren't there, then I would try it. But you're hours away. I don't have the time to drive there on the weekends. You're a busy man owning and buying companies all over the world. Not to mention for your family. Long-distance relationships rarely amount to anything. I'm old fashioned and don't know how to make this work. I don't even use dating apps."

Like most of her friends did.

"You've been doing some reading," he said, smiling.

"Hard not to," she said.

"Don't believe everything you read."

"Don't worry," she said. "I didn't see anything about you with another woman. No pictures either."

He smiled. "You wouldn't have looked if you weren't concerned about it."

"That's just another obstacle. Why doesn't someone like you have any pictures in the media with a woman?"

"Aside from being a very private person, I'm guarded. On top of that, I haven't had a lot of time to commit to someone."

"And there you are answering everything for me without me opening my mouth."

"That was in the past," he said. "This is here and now. I'm going to make the time."

"You want me to believe that at thirty-six years old, you're going to make the time to be with *me*?"

"Yes, I do," he said.

"Sorry," she said. "It doesn't make sense. If you want me to even consider trying you've got to convince me. You have to make me believe, and right now, you jumping on your jet to talk to me in person isn't doing it. Not when a month from now. Probably even a week from now, I might not even be able to get a return text from you within hours."

Not that she was a needy person, but she didn't want to go days without talking to someone.

Not someone she had this much of a connection to.

It'd just hurt way too much to open herself up to giving him a chance and have it fail the way she knew it would.

"Let's make a deal," he said.

"I don't play games."

"Then give me a month," he said.

"A month?" she asked.

"Yes. They say you need thirty days to form a habit. Give me one month to prove to you that I can make this work. And you have to put some effort into it too. It can't just be me."

If he was willing to do that, then she was willing to prove him wrong.

There was just no way this was going to work.

"I can put the effort in. I mean it's only thirty days. But I have to know, are we keeping this a secret?"

She watched as he looked as if he was thinking it through. "Not from your family if you don't want to," he said.

"What about your family?" she asked, lifting her chin. "From the media, definitely. I don't want my pictures anywhere linked to you."

He frowned. "Why is that?"

"Because I don't need my name dragged through anything. I don't want to be looked into. I don't want people comparing us or feeling sorry for me or saying I'm some gold digger. Or that it didn't last like everyone will think. Did you even think of those things?"

"I have," he said. "Part of the reason I'm private."

"Which means from your family then?" she asked. "How

is that going to be possible if you're working all the time? Don't you have to tell them where you are?"

He laughed. "I don't report to anyone. But if you want my family to know, then I'm all in for it."

She frowned this time. That didn't go the way she thought it might.

In her mind, if he didn't want to tell his family then maybe he wasn't all in.

The fact he gave in so easily wasn't what she expected.

"I didn't think you'd agree," she said.

"Because you're looking for everything to go wrong before you look for something to go right," he said. "I'd like to think everything we did in Aruba was right."

She couldn't argue with that.

"I want you to meet my sister and her fiancé while you're here," she said suddenly.

He looked at his watch. "How do you know they aren't busy?"

"My sister has to go to work in a few hours. She's probably eating dinner and relaxing with Christian. I'm sure they are home. They don't live that far. Or do you need to go back to the airport?"

"I've got a few hours," he said.

"You're giving in awfully fast," she said.

He laughed. "Is it helping to convince you?"

"I just don't know what to think," she said. Now that he wasn't being pushy, he was the guy she'd fallen for.

"Don't think at all," he said. He reached for her and pulled her onto his lap. "I want you to feel. Just that. That's what I've been doing for days. Why can't that be enough?"

"It's never enough," she said. "A relationship can't all be about sex."

"I didn't say anything about sex," he said softly. "It's what you make me feel inside."

He put her hand to his chest, his covering hers and their fingers entwining. Those words were her deciding factor to give this a try.

What harm could it do?

13

HANDLE THIS SITUATION

"It's nice to meet you," Liz said to West thirty minutes later.

He was shocked that he'd been able to get Abby to go along with the thirty-day trial.

Hell, he was willing to try anything and for a guy that took what he wanted in life, that was saying a lot.

He didn't want to think he didn't like being told no. It couldn't be that.

It was her. The way she made him feel.

West didn't want to give that up without seeing what more there was to come.

But he knew he had to handle this situation differently.

She was skittish and had trust issues. The fact she found out about him the way she had hadn't helped.

But he'd been honest days ago that he couldn't think of any other way for her to find out.

In his mind, they'd still be in this boat, even if he'd told her in person.

"You too," he said. "I've heard a lot about you."

Liz grinned. She was in her scrubs and he knew she was

getting ready to go to work soon. "I've heard about you. My sister failed to mention that you called her."

He turned to look at the two sisters eying each other.

"There wasn't much to say," she said.

"I think considering West is standing here, there is a lot to say. And please, excuse the construction. Christian is in the shower and will be down in a few minutes. He's been working on the house."

Abby had told him that Christian was an engineer and his family owned a construction company.

When he'd looked into Abby and tried to find her address, he'd done a search on her sister and the fiancé. He figured he had the basic information.

The Butlers had started a development called Paradise Place. He found that funny, but driving through it just now on the way to Liz's house, it seemed like a great place to grow up.

Liz's house was older, he could see. But it was huge with a lot of character and it appeared they were doing some major renovations.

"I didn't expect to have him show up on my doorstep tonight," Abby said.

"I'm a man of surprises," he said.

"Please," Liz said. "Come into the kitchen. I was just getting ready to cook dinner."

"Sorry to put you out," he said. "We can go out to dinner."

"No," Liz said. "It's fine. I've got plenty. I'm only making burgers."

Abby started to laugh. "Real beef, West."

"What am I missing?" Liz asked.

"West likes beef. When we were in Aruba there was

more fish than anything else. He had to get some sent in special on a day trip we had."

"I'm with him." He assumed this man was Christian Butler. They were about the same height, even build.

Christian was smiling, but he knew it was guarded.

He'd be the same way if the roles were reversed and Christian was the stranger coming in.

"Christian likes anything I'm cooking for him," Liz said. "Can we get you a drink? Something strong?"

"You're going to be questioned," Abby said. "Be thankful I didn't invite my father over. He doesn't know about you."

Which told him she might not have wanted her father to know what she'd done on her trip.

He followed them through the massive downstairs, into the back of the house. Here the kitchen was new and modern but still had a lot of character. He was positive it was recently done.

"I'll take a beer," he said. "If you've got it." Christian went to the fridge and pulled out two beers and held them up in question. "Whatever you pour I'll drink."

Christian moved past the fridge and got a of couple glasses, poured them and handed one over.

"I'm only finding out what is going on," Christian said. "As of fifteen minutes ago."

"Oh," he said.

Liz shrugged. "I didn't know if Abby wanted me to share. She gave the impression nothing else was going to happen and I didn't want to pry."

West didn't like hearing that.

"It seems your sister might need some convincing."

"Abby knows her mind," Liz said.

"I told West that."

"I think your sister is shy," he said. "She wasn't last week."

He turned and saw her face get red. "Thanks for that."

"It's not what I meant," he said. "Just that I thought we had a lot of fun together. I had no intention of saying goodbye and never seeing her again. She assumed that, but I was pretty clear otherwise."

Christian looked at Abby. "Is that true?"

"He did say it," she conceded.

"Do you want to see him again?" Christian asked.

"He wouldn't be standing here if the answer was no."

West was glad she was being honest at least.

"That solves that part," Christian said. "As I said, I just found out a few things. Tell me about yourself."

He snorted. It felt like a job interview, but he wasn't going to be put off.

"I'm not sure what you know or want to know," he said.

"I'm hearing I can find out a lot about you online," Christian said. "Tell me something I can't."

This was harder than he imagined it'd be.

He'd never been quizzed before by anyone other than his own family.

Most knew a lot about him.

Nor was he trying to impress them.

But he needed to impress Abby's sister and future brother-in-law if he wanted a chance.

"My brother Braylon is a few years younger than me. I'd already gotten my MBA on scholarships while working several jobs. Braylon was in college and finishing law school. When he graduated, he could have had his choice of multiple job offers. He said he wanted to work with me. That I'd need him to be where I am. He was right. I couldn't have done what I have without him."

"You didn't tell me that," Abby said. "I just assumed he came to work with you afterward. Or a few years ago."

"No," he said. "I'd had a few investments at that point. Businesses I took a risk on. They were paying off. I was paying a lawyer when I needed one. I didn't have a lot to offer him at the time. We all had loans for school."

"But loyalty is why he stayed by your side," Christian said.

"Yes," he said. "Our family is close. Close enough that my mother kicked my butt and played me to go on that vacation because I guess I'd lost sight of the important things and my siblings all saw it but me."

"That's two things he shared," Abby said. "Happy?"

West held back his grin. Sounded like she was sticking up for him now.

"It's not about me being happy," Liz said. "It's about you."

"We agreed to try this for thirty days."

"That's oddly specific," Christian said, grinning.

"A month," he clarified. "Some months have thirty-one days."

Abby laughed at him. "Or twenty-eight. I think thirty was being fair."

"We know you're all about being fair," he said.

"That's right," she said. "Don't forget it. Just because my bank account is more like your loose change doesn't mean I don't have a voice."

"Heard," he said.

Liz grinned. "I'm going to throw the burgers on the grill. I've got some potato salad made and I'll toss some French fries in the air fryer. Abby isn't a fan of mayonnaise."

"It's gross," she said.

"Something I didn't know about you either," he said.

"There is a lot you don't know about me," she said.

"Then I look forward to learning."

At eight they were back at Abby's. "Thanks for being such a good sport about everything. You never did say what you were doing tonight. Do you have a hotel or are you flying back?"

"I was going to fly back. My pilot is waiting," he said. "He can get a hotel or he can stay on the jet. There is a bedroom."

"You let your pilot stay in your room?"

"Just because someone works for me doesn't mean I inconvenience them."

"You mean like them not knowing when they'd be home?" she asked.

"That is part of the job they are paid well for. I didn't have my flight attendant for a short flight. Trust me when I tell you those who work for me in positions I depend on are compensated heavily."

"I can only imagine," she said.

He pulled her into his arms. "The question is, am I going back to the airport or do we have the night together to talk some more? Maybe figure out the next step? We can't wait too long to get moving with only thirty days."

"Considering you put yourself out there," she said, "you can stay tonight and we can talk. I'll take the couch."

He made sure he showed no reaction to that statement.

"I'd argue I'd do it, but I don't think I'd fit."

She kissed him on the lips. "Or you want the chance to convince me to go to the bedroom with you."

"Do I have a shot of convincing you?"

She grinned. "You wouldn't be here if you didn't."

He picked her up and carried her to her room.

14

LESS INTIMIDATING

It felt like a dream when Abby rolled over the next day and saw West under the covers in her double bed.

They barely fit together, but since he had her tucked under his arm the whole time, it hadn't mattered all that much.

How could so much have changed in such a short period of time?

She looked at the clock in her room and saw it was five. She had another hour before her alarm went off, but West said he had to be to the airport early to get back to his office. That he had some explaining to do to his family.

She wanted to give him the benefit of the doubt he'd do it.

Since she agreed to fly to see him after work on Friday, she had to believe he'd let some of his siblings know.

She was aware that Braylon and Laken lived close by. Foster wasn't that far away. Maybe she'd meet one or more of them over the weekend.

They hadn't gotten that far yet.

One day at a time was how she was going to plan this out.

She threw the covers back and slid out of bed and made her way to the bathroom.

She showered and dried her hair as quickly as possible. When she opened her bathroom door, she smelled coffee.

"Morning," he said.

"Morning to you," she said, moving close to get a kiss. Her hand came up and rubbed against the growth of beard since he shaved yesterday morning. "I like this on you. It makes you less intimidating."

"I don't want you to feel intimidated by me at all," he said.

"It's hard not to," she said. "But that is my problem and not yours."

"It shouldn't be a problem at all, but we'll work on it together."

He gave her another kiss, then took his coffee with him into the bathroom with his bag. She found it funny he had a change of clothes with him in the car but had said he would have gotten a hotel if he had to. He tried not to sleep on the jet if he could avoid it but had.

She was positive his jet was probably more comfortable than her bed or any hotel room.

When he came out of the bathroom, she had some scrambled eggs made and toast.

"Nothing fancy but the least I could do was feed you," she said.

"Thanks," he said. "Sorry for getting you up so early. Once I get to the airport they will get ready to take off."

"Are you going to work like that?" she asked.

He had on nice pants, a button-down shirt, that was

unbuttoned a few and shoes on his feet. Brown leather ones that looked like they could be sneakers by the soles.

She was positive his outfit today, however casual, probably cost more than her car payment.

"Yes," he said.

"A driver will get you at the airport and bring you there when you land?" she asked.

"I don't make a habit of driving around much. I have a driver take me places but do have a car. I can drive, as you know."

"What kind of car do you have?" she asked.

He lifted his eyebrow at her. "I have a few. Does it matter?"

"I guess not," she said.

She wasn't sure why she was asking.

"I've got a Jag," he said. "And a Range Rover. Modest, all things considered."

"I guess," she said, laughing. "I think the rented Mercedes you had was high end and that is pretty much normal for a lot of people."

"It's only a car," he said.

She wouldn't say anything else. She had to stop it.

Maybe she was the one making a bigger deal out of things, as he said.

"It is," she said.

He finished his breakfast fairly fast. "I hate to run. You start work at eight?"

"I do. I get there a little before and I'm done at four thirty."

"I hate to leave, but I'll see you tomorrow night, right? No changing your mind when I leave?"

She was surprised he seemed unsure of things, but she supposed he had a reason.

"No," she said. "I won't. Just have to wrap my head around the fact that I've been on two vacations my whole life. I've flown four times. There and back on both vacations and they were years apart. And now I'm going to be flying again in less than a week from returning."

"Think of it as faster than driving. No long waits in the airport."

"That is something to get used to too. Where to go and all."

He'd told her where to go on Friday and would have it all cleared for her. It was going to feel odd, but she had to get all those feelings out and over with now.

It'd be hard to move forward with anything if everything they did together in the next month she was feeling unsure.

How could she open herself up to giving him a chance if she was nervous about being looked at and judged?

"You'll be fine," he said. "Trust me. But I do need to run."

She kissed him. Not a quick one, but a long drawn out one. "I'm not a clingy person."

"Neither am I," he said.

"But would it be horrible to say that I'm going to miss you even though I'll see you again soon?"

He smiled at her. The charming smile he'd given her so much of when they were on a tropical island and she started to think this might not be so bad.

"Not at all."

Abby watched him leave and then got ready for work. She was earlier than normal and just decided to go in. No reason not to.

She wasn't shocked when her sister called her though before eight.

"Are you just getting out of work?" she asked Liz.

"I am. I'm driving home now. Tell me what happened last night?"

"I'm not telling you everything," she said, laughing.

"The sound of your voice says it all. I'm glad to know you're giving him a chance."

"Why do you want me to?" she asked.

Liz was guarded more than Abby was. She was positive it had to do with Liz's ex-husband, Tanner.

"I think we all deserve to find happiness," Liz said.

"Thanks," she said. "But I have no idea what is going to come out of this. I'm not holding my breath. It doesn't seem like the normal progression of dating I'm used to. I don't like feeling out of my element and this is another universe."

"He seems genuine," Liz said. "And traveling alone was not normal for you, but you did, and look at what good came of it. Taking some risks isn't a bad thing."

She sighed. Her sister was right as always. "He did seem genuine. I mean what you saw of him last night was how he was with me all last week. I was happy to see it, as it was not the person who called me on the phone."

"That's good," Liz said.

"I know. But I'm positive I'm going to see a different side to him soon. I'm flying on his *jet* to see him this weekend."

Liz laughed. "I can't wait to hear how that is."

"I'm nervous."

"Don't be. Be you. It seems to me you made an impression on him doing that so far."

"I can't compete in his world," she said.

"I don't know that he wants you to," Liz said. "Maybe at the heart of it, he's just like us. His upbringing and family. Money can and does change people a lot and you'll find out if that is the case with West or not."

"I hope it's not," she said. "I really would hate myself if I went there and found he was an ass to his employees. He already admitted the vacation was because of the way he was treating his family."

"Come on," Liz said. "You know that isn't the case, right? His mother told him to cut the crap as you said and he listened to her. Didn't you tell me that he apologized to his siblings too or something?"

"Yeah. He touched on that briefly, but I didn't understand what he was saying and didn't ask."

"I think you are looking for excuses to not have this work before you give it a chance to see if it can."

"I've never been that way," she said. "Why am I now?"

"I think you're scared," Liz said. "I know that feeling. I felt it when Christian came back into my life. I didn't want to blow it, but I'd been hurt before. I had to put me first and if that meant hurting him, I had to decide what carried more weight."

"Christian understood it all," she said.

"That's right. He did. Christian isn't the only great guy out there."

"Good words to remember," she said. "I'll let you get some sleep."

"I just pulled into the driveway. First...are you saying anything to Dad?"

"Not yet. I want to see what happens this weekend. Then I'll decide. Maybe one trip there will be enough for me to know it's not going to work. I mean, you can want something badly, but if you're uncomfortable or anxious about it, it's not healthy either."

"No," Liz said softly. "It's not. And I'm sorry if you feel that way. I won't pressure you. You know that. I never would. If it's meant, West will understand and try to ease that feeling for you."

"If he can," she said. "I can't let someone else do that. I need to do it myself."

"No one says you have to be alone," Liz said. "Remember that too. We all need to learn to love ourselves in order to love another person."

She laughed. "I didn't know you were changing fields from nursing to counseling."

"I'm not," Liz said. "Just some big sister advice from the mistakes I've made."

"You've always given me good advice and I appreciate it. I'll never be able to repay you."

"I don't need any payment," Liz said. "I just want you happy."

"I want you happy too. I know you are, which is why you keep saying it to me," she said.

She hung up with her sister after that.

There was no reason to talk about love anymore. It was way too soon for that.

More so because she knew if she opened herself up, she could fall and fall hard.

She'd done it before in her life and knew how much it hurt when you put your trust in someone else and they failed you.

She wasn't sure she could survive it again.

"You're here early, Abby."

She shook her head to clear her thoughts to see Carly standing in her doorway. A coworker she didn't often like talking to because it was always petty and gossiping.

"Still trying to catch up," she said.

"Must be nice to win a trip and come back all relaxed. Guess you are luckier than the rest of us."

She ignored that. "Is there something I can help you with?"

Carly walked in. "Wait until I tell you what I heard last night about the manager in store number fourteen."

She kept her eyes from rolling. It was always like this. She'd listen but not comment. Most likely nothing happened to warrant HR getting involved and it was merely juice for Carly's grapevine cup more than anything.

Maybe she could just zone out and think about West with a smile on her face.

Yeah, she'd do that instead.

15

PLAN FOR ANYTHING

Abby was used to looking over her shoulder in life. What she wasn't used to was doing it in a place where she didn't feel as if she belonged.

If it wasn't for the fact that she'd given her name at a desk for her flight on West's jet, she would have felt as if this was a dream.

"Abby Sherman?"

She turned to see an older woman in a black pantsuit coming her way. Not a traditional flight suit, but more like a business-style one that was comfy to wear.

How could a business suit be comfy?

"That's me," she said, standing up.

"I'm Susie Blackwell. I'll be your flight attendant for this trip. West said this is the first time you've flown on a private jet."

"It is," she said. "I haven't even flown first class before."

Susie smiled gently. "I can assure you first class will never measure up to this. We can board and I'll give you a tour. Then we'll get ready for takeoff when the pilot is given permission. We've got about twenty minutes at least."

Abby grabbed her luggage and pulled it along. She had no idea what to pack. West hadn't given her any indication of what they were doing this weekend. Just said plan for anything.

Yeah, in his eyes he could just do that. Not her. It's not like she had fancy dresses or shoes and wasn't sure she wanted to even do those things that would require it.

She had dark jeans on with one of her dress shirts tucked in. Ankle boots on her feet. This was what she'd worn to work and hoped it was okay. She had no idea who she was going to meet right away and jeans with sneakers might come off wrong.

Then she told herself to cut it out. She was who she was. She couldn't be anyone else.

No amount of polish or shine was going to make brass look like gold and it'd only force her to run in the other direction. West was going to have to understand that early on.

They walked out of the building and toward a plane that looked too big to be a private jet. Good lord, she wasn't even sure what she had in mind, but it wasn't this. This looked like a plane she'd buy tickets on to travel. Maybe not the biggest, but big enough.

"This is West's plane?" she asked when they walked to the staircase leading up.

"It is," Susie said. "I know it's a lot to take in. You haven't even seen the best part of it."

She was starting to dread this trip.

When she got to the top, she turned and looked and started to laugh.

"Oh my God. There is a living room in here. And a dining room!"

Susie patted her hand and grinned. "Conference table to seat up to twenty."

The gray leather chairs all had seatbelts in them she could see, but it looked as if all the seats by the windows were cushy recliners rather than airline chairs.

Lots of monitors that were attached and could swivel for a better view or out of the way. Must be people worked a lot on this plane.

The living room on one end where she walked had a massive TV mounted on the wall. Like one you'd see in the showroom of an electronic store that everyone wanted but no one could afford.

The sectionals around it were the same gray leather too.

"This is a lot for one person to fly in," she said.

"West doesn't often fly alone. When he goes on business trips he can take large groups with him. Let me show you to the other side."

The cockpit must be past the conference table. Now they were turning right to the back of the plane.

"How many bathrooms are there?" She'd just passed two.

"Four," Susie said. "Two for all the guests to share, one for staff, and then West has his own suite."

"Staff," she asked. "How many staff?"

"A pilot and copilot most times and myself. If there are a lot of people on board or a longer trip we've got a chef and wait staff."

They'd just passed the kitchen she looked into. It was nicer and bigger than most kitchens in a small restaurant.

"Good lord, this could be someone's house."

Susie grinned. "Yes. There have been times when we've hit bad weather and have had to stay overnight. No reason to even get a hotel. The sectionals turn into beds if need be, most of the chairs recline back to make sleeping easier."

They moved to the back and a door was opened.

"West's bedroom?" she asked. If the bedroom looked like this on his jet she could only imagine what his penthouse would be like.

"Yes," Susie said. "There is a bath through there."

She walked a bit and popped her head into what she'd consider to be a dream bathroom with a walk-in shower and soaker tub. *On a jet!*

The closet was on her right and she noticed a few suits and other clothes in there. She supposed he liked to be prepared for anything.

Guess when you were a billionaire you could be.

"This is too much," she said softly.

"Relax," Susie said. "Don't let it get to you. West is a down-to-earth guy when you get to know him."

She wondered if Susie was aware of her and West's relationship.

"Do you know why I'm going to see him?"

Susie patted her hand. "I'm kind of like a bartender to West. We talk and it goes no further. I know he met you in Aruba and now you two are going to try a long-distance relationship. That is the extent of my knowledge though."

She didn't believe that one bit but wasn't going to dispute it.

She nodded and followed Susie out.

"Do I just sit anywhere?" She was feeling awfully lonely in this much space.

"You can," Susie said. "Do you want to meet the pilots?"

"Sure," she said. "I've never been in a cockpit before."

She walked the length of the plane thinking she could

do laps in here for a workout on longer flights and then had to stop herself from giggling over the thought.

The pilots were in their seats. Both shook hands with her and then went back to doing their job.

"You can take a seat wherever you're comfortable in one of the chairs for takeoff. Once we are in flight, you can move to the couches and turn the TV on if you'd like."

"The flight isn't even an hour, right?" she asked.

"No," Susie said. "Less than."

"I'll just stay in my seat I'm sure." She ran her hand over the back of the buttery soft material. "They are nicer than what I've got in my living room."

Her face flushed when she'd said that. She supposed she was coming off like a country bumpkin at this point.

"I understand," Susie said. "It's the same for me too. I enjoy coming to work and sitting in the chairs. There are several that are massage chairs."

"Oh," she said. "Why am I not surprised?"

"If you'd like some company, we can sit together. I'll show you how to use the controls. You might be on this more than you realize."

She snorted over that comment. "I'm not sure about that," she said. "But I'd love the company."

They sat together in the middle of the plane, facing each other, buckled in and waited for takeoff.

Since it was just the two of them, there was no reason for Susie to talk into the speaker to the whole plane.

When the plane started to move, it was no different than the flight she'd taken last week other than the fact it was peaceful and it was more comfortable than any other traveling she'd ever done in her life.

Less than an hour later, she was exiting the plane. She'd been told a car would be waiting for her. She didn't expect the black town car when Susie walked her to it.

"This is one of West's cars and drivers."

"One of them?" she asked.

"He has two cars and two drivers. Obviously he doesn't use them both all the time. He doesn't do a lot of driving around the city but has another car available for employees when needed. I believe he's got one right now for him."

"Duh," she said and wished she'd kept to her inside voice and not sounded like even more of an idiot. "Sorry. This is overwhelming."

"I know," Susie said. "Consider it a convenience more than anything else."

She nodded, but when she climbed in, the last person she thought she'd see was West sitting there.

"Hey," he said.

"Oh my God," she said. "I didn't think you'd be getting me. You said a car would be waiting."

"It is," he said, leaning in for a kiss. He was in a suit and yeah...intimidating came to mind once again. But sexy at the same time. "But I'm with it. How was the flight?"

"Amazing," she said. "Everyone should fly like that."

He laughed. "I'm glad it was good. We are going to take another one."

"What?" she asked. "Where?"

"We are going to my beach house in the Hamptons. I thought you might feel more comfortable there the first time. It's about a two-hour drive or a forty-minute helicopter ride. Your choice, but we have to go to another terminal and that is too far to walk."

"Oh," she said. "I've never been in a helicopter before. Let me guess, this is your private one?"

He laughed at her. "I have a landing pad on the top of

my office building. It's easier at times to travel that way to the airport if I'm in a hurry or to come to my home here. It can be four hours in the car from my penthouse to the beach house and I do enjoy the quiet."

"Might as well fly," she said. "I'm hungry and two hours in the car would prolong that."

"I'll have dinner ready when we get there."

"Another private chef?" she asked. She hadn't even known he had a house in the Hamptons and then realized he probably had places all over the world where he could stay.

"Not like you think," he said. "I'm not out there often. Someone that I hire locally to come in when needed. I'm having dinner made there for us tonight and food for the weekend. I can and do cook when needed. I'm not that spoiled."

She looked around the car they were in and then when they stopped to get out by a helicopter.

"Yeah," she said. "Not spoiled at all."

16

ALL IN

West had thought about it since yesterday and quickly decided that having Abby in Manhattan for the first time in his penthouse might not be the best thing to do.

Bringing her to the beach again would hopefully remind her of their week together.

That did mean helicopter rides and drivers but it's not like he had to hide what he had. That would be stupid and best to put it all out there right now.

Besides, Braylon, Laken and Foster were coming out tomorrow. Braylon and Laken would fly in the helicopter and Foster was only an hour away, he'd drive.

He was going to prove to Abby that he was all in, and in order to do that, he had to let his family know.

So far, he'd only told those three, as he communicated with them the most.

He didn't think they'd say anything to the rest of his siblings or his mother. He'd asked them not to. Told them he'd talk to their mom himself to avoid getting a lecture, but he hadn't had time.

Knowing he was going to walk away from work most of this weekend meant he had been at it since four this morning. He worked until ten last night too.

But he was determined to give Abby his attention while she was here so she knew he was committed.

Once they were in the helicopter and headsets on, they took off and flew over Long Island to Mecox Bay where his private home was located on a few acres of land.

"Home for the weekend," he said, pointing to the house below. They'd land on his property, which made it all convenient.

Abby looked down. "I can't tell how big it is. I mean I'm expecting a mansion and right now we are too far up."

"Far from a mansion," he said, laughing. "But it is about forty-five hundred square feet."

"That's not much bigger than Liz's house," she said, letting out a sigh. "Though I'm sure it's nothing like hers inside."

"You'd be surprised," he said.

He loved this house for the character and the charm. It wasn't flashy and fancy like his penthouse.

He came here to relax and he wanted it to have the vibe.

"It's pretty," she said.

"You seem so shocked."

They climbed out of the helicopter, West grabbing her luggage. He had a briefcase in his hand, his black suit jacket still on, his shirt white, his pants black, no tie. He'd ditched that before he left the office but hadn't had time to change.

Then he told himself that she had to see him like he was. There could be no hiding anything at this point. It wouldn't be fair to either of them, but he wanted her to see all sides that very few ever did.

"I didn't think it looked like a beach house. A big one, but still it's got the weathered look."

"That's very common here. I wasn't going for new and modern, but it is inside."

They walked to the back door, past his infinity pool that looked out into the bay in the distance and into his weekend home.

"I could live in this room alone," she said of the sunroom they entered. The windows sprawled across the entire back with doors that opened up to the patio.

"It reminds me of Aruba," he said. "Indoor and outdoor living when the weather is nice. Not quite warm enough for it now."

"No," she said.

"Hi, Andrea," he said to the chef in his kitchen. "Smells good."

"That's what you pay me for," Andrea said. "I'll just set it all up and get out of your way."

"Thanks," he said, moving past the big white and bright kitchen that had been redone a few years ago. It's not like he entertained often, but he made sure he could if he wanted to and had the kitchen set up for caterers to come in and do their thing comfortably.

"How many bedrooms do you have here?"

"Four," he said. "The main is downstairs with a bath obviously. There are four other bathrooms in the house too. One full on this floor for guests. Then one bedroom upstairs has its own, the other two share one between them. There is a second living room upstairs over the garage as well with a small galley kitchen and bath there."

"So guests could be out of the way if they want," she said.

"Yes," he said. "I'll show you around more later if you'd like. Might as well feed you while it's still hot."

Her head was moving around to everything they passed, but she hadn't made too many comments other than she found the place pretty.

They moved to his room on the other side of the house and went through the double doors.

"The view," she said. "I stand corrected. I might never leave this room."

"It's a nice view in the morning," he said. "Better at night with the moon over the water."

"Why would anyone not want to live here full time?" she asked.

"It's more convenient for me to be in the city since I work long days and nights," he said. "But this is where I come on the weekends often."

Her hand was trailing along the white bedspread and his body had ideas of more than eating food.

It didn't seem as if he'd just seen her on Wednesday night and had his fill. He was starting to think he might never get enough of her.

"You can change if you want," she said. "Do you have a place for me to unpack? I packed more than I needed but wanted to try to be prepared for anything. That's not easy for me."

"If you want to hang anything up, there is space in the closet. There are a few empty drawers in here too."

She unzipped her bag and pulled out a black dress. He'd love to see her in that but had nothing planned for it this weekend.

She hung it up and put shoes next to it. The look on her face said she hoped she didn't have to put it on.

The rest of her clothes were jeans and shirts, leggings and T-shirts.

He wanted her to be comfortable and would make sure she was able to be while she was here so she'd come back again next week.

He grabbed a pair of jeans and a cotton shirt. He always took a shower when he got out of work but didn't want her to wait if she was hungry.

"You're eying the bathroom," she said. "Go shower if you want. I understand. I can wait a few more minutes to eat. I know you're fast."

"Thanks," he said. "Only fast in the shower though, not anything else in life."

She laughed, but he could tell she was still tense.

He went into his bathroom, undressed, showered quickly and came out to see her sitting on the bed. She had black leggings on and a fitted cotton shirt that landed at her hips.

She was thin but in good shape. Healthy.

He didn't like women who starved themselves to have a body like Abby's.

"I thought I'd wait in here for you," she said.

He held his hand out to her; she got up and moved closer to him. "Relax. I'm the same guy I was a week ago."

She laughed at him. "Yes and no. That guy didn't have a private jet and helicopter he could call up anytime he wanted."

"Yes, I did," he said.

"But I didn't know that," she said.

"And yet it didn't change anything," he said.

"It did for me."

She said it so softly that he wasn't sure he was meant to hear it so he wouldn't address it right now.

He had to tread carefully, so he only pulled her into his arms for a quick hug.

"Let's go eat."

"What did you have made?" she asked.

"Seafood casserole," he said. "Andrea would have made some pasta and vegetables with it. I just requested that. I know you like seafood. I told her the vegetables that you'd eaten already and she would have done the rest."

"I'm not a fussy eater," she said. "My father was a simple cook and then Liz took over. I did it, but I'm not as good as her."

"I'm sure you could be if you wanted to be," he said.

"I think that is part of it. I just never had to do much. My father is a pretty easy man and liked anything I put in front of him."

"It wasn't your father that you wanted to please though, was it?"

"No," she said, letting out a sigh. "Sometimes I wish I didn't tell you as much as I have."

"I don't wish that," he said. "I want to know more."

He knew she still had issues with her mother abandoning her. Letting her in again. Hoping for things that might never happen.

"That takes time," she said. "This weekend I can learn about you."

"If that is how you want it," he said.

He got plates down and put them on the island. No reason to sit in the dining room or at the table off to the side.

He wanted it cozy with just the two of them.

She found the silverware and then the two of them made their plates with the food that Andrea had left spread out.

"This is so good," she said. "I'd be fat if someone cooked for me like this."

"No, you wouldn't. You appreciate good things, but you wouldn't want it all the time," he said. "I'll be cooking the rest of the weekend. You'll have to live with that."

She laughed and bumped her shoulder next to his. "I can cook too. Maybe we can do it together."

It seemed he made the right decision not to have Andrea do much more than buy some food for him. It's not like he had all his meals prepared when he was in his penthouse either.

"We can do that," he said.

They ate their meal and they chatted about his plane and all the things she found nice about it. He was glad she didn't seem put off by it, but he could see she was trying to not be either.

They got dinner cleaned up and he pulled her into the sunroom. It was close to eight at this point. He'd been up and working since four, but that was normal for him.

Abby was yawning though.

"What are we doing?" she asked.

"We are going to sit on the couch and stare out at the water like we did before."

"Different kind of water but still beautiful," she said. "I know you've got neighbors. I saw them when we flew over. But you don't see them much here."

"Trees and distance," he said. "I don't know who they are. They don't know me. When I come here it's not to entertain. But we will be doing that tomorrow."'

He figured he might as well let her know now.

"Oh," she said. "What's going on?"

"Braylon and Laken are flying in and Foster is driving. He lives about an hour from here."

"You're introducing me to your family?"

Her voice seemed shocked. "I told you I was. Might as well do it now. It's only those three. They are the ones around. No one else knows."

"Not even your mother?" she asked.

"No. I'll tell her myself this weekend."

"While I'm here?" she asked.

"I'd rather not," he said dryly.

"Why?" she asked.

He ran his finger over the crease in her eyebrows.

"Because she'll want to talk to you."

She smiled. "I don't care," she said.

"I might care. Let's do it my way. We can work up to my mother slowly. Unless you want me to meet your father."

"Not yet," she said quickly.

He wouldn't be hurt by that. He'd met her sister so that would be good enough.

17

OUT OF HER REACH

It seemed the day to get hit with all sorts of surprises and news.

First the two flights here to a house she didn't even know West owned.

Then the private chef with a fabulous dinner.

Followed up with the information she'd be meeting three of his siblings.

When she agreed to this weekend she didn't know what to expect.

It definitely wasn't any of this.

She was glad they were here though.

The bright lights and noise of Manhattan weren't things she thought she'd enjoy.

It didn't sound appealing to her either.

This place, this was much more her style even if it was out of her reach.

It just felt comfortable. Relaxing.

Almost serene.

She needed that right now after the rollercoaster of the past ten days.

If she thought of this as part of a vacation again, it was easier in her mind.

To distract them both, she put her hand on his thigh and moved it up and down.

He leaned in and kissed her neck.

"What are you doing?"

"I think it's pretty obvious," she said. "If weekends are when we get to see each other, then we have to take advantage of the time, don't you think?"

"I do," he said. "But that isn't the only reason I want to see you."

Most men didn't say that. Or think it. Maybe not even believe it.

She had to remind herself that West wasn't like most men. Not even close.

"I know," she said. "But we haven't had much time together and there are so many things I'd like to do."

"Oh really?" he asked.

"Yep," she said.

Her hand moved to the button on his jeans and undid it, then lowered the zipper.

She freed his cock and stroked him up and down a few times, a little dew gathering at the tip.

She moved away from his side and got on her knees in front of him on the couch, her back to the water.

"Now this is one hell of a view," he said.

She looked up and smiled at him, then dipped her head down and covered his cock fully, wetting it and then sliding her hand up and down with a few more strokes.

When she lifted her eyes again, his head was back on the couch and not really watching her but rather enjoying what was happening.

That was even better in her mind.

She went back to what she was doing, licking up and down and around the tip, then covering him completely.

She started to suck and he let out a groan, then pushed her shoulders back a bit.

"What's wrong?" she asked.

"Just need a break," he said.

"Oh. I don't want to give you a break though."

He moaned this time. Not one in pleasure but more like in frustration. "I'm not used to being told no."

She laughed. "Well then. Looks like you're getting out of your comfort zone tonight too. Seems fair to me, don't you think?"

He squinted one eye at her. "Brat."

She smirked and then went down on him again, this time moving faster.

Harder.

More intense.

Might as well.

He was squirming on the couch and trying to give himself some room away from her, but she had a grip on his cock and was stroking and sucking and not letting him move.

"Fuck!" he said and he started to come in her mouth.

She'd been expecting it. Normally she'd stop at that point, as it wasn't her favorite thing to do, though she'd done it in the past.

She didn't even think to stop with West and wasn't sure why.

She swallowed what she could so she didn't make a mess and then leaned back, her hand moving slowly on him still, more coming out but only in dribbles.

She actually just liked to watch it and couldn't pull her eyes away.

"You okay?" he asked.

"Sure," she said. "I should ask you that. You sound like you're out of breath."

"I feel that way," he said.

Before she could comment though she found herself picked up and put on the couch and him on his knees in front of her.

She'd let out a gasp at the move and then was more stunned when her leggings were yanked down fast.

"Whoa," she said. "I didn't know you could move that quickly."

"You said you wanted to learn more about me this weekend and I guess this is going to be part of it."

He spread her legs as wide as they could go with her leggings around her ankles.

She kicked one leg free since she didn't have shoes on and he took that as an invitation to dive right in.

His hands spread her inner thighs wide, his tongue came out and licked the length of her.

She'd done the same to him, so she expected the payback.

But he didn't stop there.

Nope, he put two fingers in her and started to pump them in and out while his lips found her swollen bud.

He was sucking and thrusting and then just stopped, moved his fingers inside of her and was doing something that she felt on her inner walls.

Whatever the hell it was had her screeching out his name and coming so hard and fast she hadn't known that was possible.

He didn't stop though like she had, he just kept going

until she literally thought her body was going to split in two with exhaustion.

"You need to stop," she said, gasping.

"Did I hurt you?" he asked, removing his fingers and moving back.

"Only my pride that I couldn't go longer," she said.

He laughed and moved back to the couch, his jeans had been adjusted but not fastened. She lifted up so she could pull her leggings back in place and he positioned her to sit on his lap.

"We've got all weekend," he said.

"Not if we've got guests," she said.

"They won't be here until late morning and will fly out after dinner. Braylon doesn't like the quiet here. Laken has to fly out for work on Sunday and Foster doesn't care for people all that much."

"Your sister sounds like she works more than you," she said. "That's not nice of you."

"It's her choice," he said. "I don't tell her how to do her job."

"You don't?" she asked. "I find that hard to believe."

He sighed. "I tell her what I want and the results I'm looking for. How she accomplishes it, it's her choice. She has a team under her and she chooses to do more rather than delegate."

"Maybe she wants to make her big brother proud and let him know that he made the right choice putting her in that position."

He frowned at her. "I am proud of her."

"Does she know it?" she asked. "Do you tell her?"

"Are you going to sound like my mother now?" he asked, tugging on her hair.

"No. Sorry. Just that I guess I know a bit about wanting to make someone proud."

He rubbed his hand up and down her back. "You made me proud just now."

"That was easy," she said, laughing.

"No," he said. "I don't think it is. And it has nothing to do with sex and everything to do with getting out of your comfort zone and giving me a chance."

Abby smiled softly. She knew he was bending over backward for her right now and didn't want that.

Her hand came up to his cheek, rubbing his light beard. "If you don't like this you can get rid of it."

"I thought you liked it?" he asked.

"I do find it sexy, but the whisker burns are a bit itchy now," she said. "I know you don't always have facial hair and you scratch it a lot."

"I can give or take it. On the weekends I let it go so it's fine. It will be gone on Monday."

"Then let it be gone this weekend too. This isn't going to work if we are worrying that we can't be ourselves."

"You're right. I'm trying to ease you into this."

"Don't," she said. "I mean it's all a shock and I appreciate coming here first. I really do. But I want you to be who you are, not who you think I want you to be."

"I am being myself," he said. "It might stun my siblings tomorrow so don't judge."

"Why will it stun them?" she asked. "If you're being yourself they should be used to it."

"They are used to it outside of the work environment. When we have time to get together. But around anyone that isn't family, they don't see me that way."

"Why are you guarded?"

"Private," he said. "There are always eyes on me and I like keeping a part of my life away from that."

"Meaning me?" she asked. Which could be why they were here and not in Manhattan where there would be more eyes.

"No," he said. "Well, yes. I want you for myself, but more importantly, I don't want to scare you away. I'm not going to lie and say that the longer this goes on, the greater the chance it's going to be leaked. You might see your name out there somewhere."

"I don't want that," she said. "Not the attention."

"I know," he said. "I'm sorry about that. I'm going to try to shield you as much as I can. My family will too. But I don't want to tell you it's not going to happen when it will at some point."

"One day at a time," she said.

"Good attitude to have," he said, hugging her tight.

18

SCARED SILLY

"Where is she?" Laken asked him around eleven the next morning.

Those were the first words out of his sister's mouth when she and Braylon came in the back door.

"Taking a shower. She worked out this morning with me."

West tried to get exercise in daily if he could, he just didn't have a set time.

Most times it helped him think, so if he was working something out, he took a break at home and then went back to what was tripping him up.

For the first time, his personal life was the thing making him think twice about everything.

He said he was going to lift weights and Abby said she'd like to work out with him if he was fine with it.

Of course he was. It just let them spend more time together.

They didn't even talk, just comments now and again.

He had the TV on some music videos and she was

focused on that while she walked on the treadmill and he lifted weights.

Then she got off the treadmill and started to lift when he went to shower.

He let her go because he knew she was nervous about meeting his siblings today.

"You don't like anyone working out with you," Braylon said. "You listen to your music and zone out to think."

"He did that with me," Abby said, walking into the room. "Which was good because I was focused on him."

He didn't expect her to say that and was thrilled that she did.

"I'm Laken," his sister said, moving forward. "And boy are we thrilled to meet you."

"You are?" she asked. "I'm scared silly to meet you guys."

"Don't let Laken intimidate you," Braylon said. "She's harmless."

His sister snorted. "I don't think anyone has ever said I was harmless."

"It's hard to be a woman in a powerful position and field," Abby said. "I know. I mean I don't personally, but I see it with my bosses."

Laken grinned. "West told us that you work in HR. Not the most favorable department in any company."

"No," she said. "I try to always be the nice one so people feel they can talk to me. Someone has to be the bad guy, but I try not to let it be me."

"Unlike me," West said. "Everyone thinks I'm the bad guy."

"It's because of all that noise you are surrounded by," Foster said, coming in the back door. "And the people. I'd be all up in everyone's face if I had to deal with that daily."

"And my last brother of the day you will meet. This is Foster. Foster, Abby Sherman."

"Nice to meet you," Foster said. His brother was the most unkempt though he had a race with Rowan. They had longer hair that was always in need of a cut. A shave was usually on the list of things too, but he couldn't say much about that when he still had some facial hair going.

He was going to shave it off but then decided to wait until Monday. No reason to do it today. He still felt it might make Abby comfortable and he'd continue for the day.

"It's nice to meet you all," Abby said. "I'm not sure what West told you about me other than we met in Aruba. I just hope that you don't think poorly of that."

He wasn't sure why she'd say that and then saw the blush fill her face.

Why hadn't he thought this through more?

"No one thinks that," he said. "Right?"

He was looking at his siblings and they were smirking at him.

"Nope," Braylon said. "It's more like we need to see what pull you've got on him. West doesn't tell anyone he's dating when he is. If he even does. The fact you just met and he told us about you is...interesting."

His siblings were going to make this harder on him, he could see it.

"Interesting how?" Abby asked. "And there isn't anything special about me."

"Sure, there is," Laken said.

"Don't do this, Abby," he said. "We talked about it. I met your sister and you are meeting mine. Or one of them. And a few brothers. What did we say? Thirty days."

Foster looked at Braylon. He hadn't had a chance to fill Foster in on that.

Braylon had no problem with doing it in front of Abby.

"Abby isn't sure she wants to be exposed to this life. West has to convince her. He has thirty days to try. You know how he is."

Foster laughed. "His 'thirty days to form a habit' bull-crap he used to tell us when we were younger?"

"Assholes," West said.

His siblings all looked shocked he'd said that in front of Abby. He wasn't one to lose his cool, but when he did, it was *only* family.

Abby laughed. "I didn't think it was something he just came up with. But maybe you can understand the most, Foster. I heard you're a hermit."

Braylon and Laken laughed. "I like her," Laken said. "You give it to him."

"I'm sorry," she said and blushed more. "I didn't mean an insult. I just was repeating what West said."

"It wasn't an insult. We bust on Foster all the time about it. My siblings will be the first to tell you that I give them the flexibility to thrive the best way they can. Don't make me out to be a jerk," he said to Laken.

"You're used to being looked at as the jerk," Laken said. "We know the truth, though."

"I don't give a crap about anyone else thinking it. I do care about what Abby thinks."

"I don't think you're a jerk," Abby said. "I think you're very kind and considerate and you're trying more than most men would with me. I think a lot in your position would just move on from my insecurities and find another woman to fawn all over them. It's just not me."

Foster started to laugh even harder. "I do like you. But West doesn't like anyone fawning over him. Maybe that is the pull, Laken?"

"It must be," his sister said.

"I need a beer," West said.

"Get me one too," Braylon said.

"I'll help," Abby said and moved into the kitchen with him. "I don't think this is going the way you want it to, is it?"

"It's going exactly the way I thought it would," he said, frowning.

She giggled. "But you don't like it?"

"I'm not used to being ganged up on," he said.

"Because you're the boss," she said. "They know that and respect it, but today you're just their big brother. Maybe you should feel good about the fact they can separate the two."

He pulled her in close for another hug. "I should. I guess I will. I don't think of those things and you make me. My mother will love you."

She stiffened in his arms and he knew that was the wrong thing to say.

Or at least too soon to say it.

"I'm not so sure how my father will feel about you," she said honestly.

"Why?" he asked.

She shrugged. "I'm the baby. I think he's going to be protective of me regardless of any man I meet."

He sighed. "And because he knows you well and will worry you're going to get hurt."

"Yeah," she said softly. "But people can't be protected their whole lives either. It's all good. I can handle it and protect myself."

Which wasn't what he wanted to hear. That maybe she was going to keep a part of herself locked away that he'd have to chisel through even more.

Nope. He didn't think so. He could read her well, her emotions were easy to spot and understand.

"No reason to talk about this today. If you want to help me put some snacks out, we can do that."

"Why don't we gather everything for lunch? When people have food in their mouths they talk less. It can give everyone a chance to warm up."

Good idea.

Since he was only serving sandwiches for lunch, he and Abby pulled out the platter with the meats and cheese and the two salads that she'd made this morning.

Braylon came in to get his beer. "You're slacking off serving me."

"I've never served you before," he said. "But your legs aren't broken and you made your way in here just fine."

"Did Andrea put this all together this morning? What is she cooking today?"

"She's not here," he said. "Abby and I did this and we are cooking dinner later."

"You're cooking for yourself?" Foster asked, moving in. "It's not going to be grilled hot dogs is it?"

West laughed. "It's been a long time since I grilled hot dogs for dinner for everyone when Mom was working."

"My father did that too," Abby said. "Or I did it because it was easy for us. But no, West has a pork loin and we are going to cook that and figure out the sides as we go."

"Yum," Laken said. "I like anything I don't have to get on the run or cook myself. I'd offer to help, but I might burn down West's kitchen and he's a bit of a neat freak."

"Laken is a slob. I'm normal."

"West is right," Braylon said. "Laken throws things around the kitchen as if she is running from one thing to the next. She only starts fires because she's not paying attention."

"You had a fire in the kitchen?" Abby asked.

"When I was sixteen," Laken said. "But no one lets me live it down."

"You have to take the good with the bad in this family," he said. "Learn to live with it."

"We all have," Foster said. "Looks like you are too."

19

CUSHIONING THE BLOW

"How come you're not saying anything?" Abby asked her father on Sunday afternoon.

She'd thought she'd be home later than she was, but West decided to go see his mother and was just dropping her off in Albany and then flying on.

She shook her head over this, but what was she going to say about it? In her mind it still didn't seem real. People she was around didn't fly anywhere they wanted when they wanted.

"What am I supposed to say, Abigail Rose?"

Oh no. The full name.

"You're just staring a me."

"Maybe it's because I'm trying to wrap my head around the fact that my youngest daughter went away for a week alone, met a stranger, spent time with him and then came back to find out he wasn't who he said he was. Then she flew to spend the weekend with him."

She was just slammed with embarrassment and shame over that statement.

This was what she wanted to avoid.

Her father being disappointed in her.

"He never lied about who he was. I mean he told me his name and a lot about his family. Even where he lived and grew up. He just didn't tell me he was a billionaire. I mean that would be kind of crass, don't you think?"

She knew she'd have to defend West but didn't think it'd be this soon.

And when those words were out of her mouth, she realized the truth of it and had to cut him some slack that he hadn't told her.

"That's not the point," her father argued.

"What is the point? This is no different than meeting someone online and having a long-distance relationship. By air, it's less than an hour."

Her father just shook his head.

"You don't meet men that way though," her father said. "Not online. I've heard it a bunch of times. You want to meet the person face to face or talk to them before you go further." Her father ran his hands through his gray hair. "I can't believe you flew there on a private jet. You could have been in danger."

"No," she said. "Cut me some slack. I'm not that naive. And I did meet him face to face. I spent days with him talking and getting to know him as if I met him in a bar here."

"Yes," her father said. "You are naive. You've always looked at life through rose-colored glasses. You get your hopes up with unrealistic expectations and no amount of cushioning the blow stops the hurt."

She knew her father was thinking about her mother.

That he'd tried so hard to make it easier for his daughters.

To protect them from everything that happened.

It didn't work.

She still had hopes her mother would come back for her.

Would just turn around and be fixed with a daily pill.

That life could be normal.

It never happened and it never would.

She'd learned it the hard way and had to accept her mother would never be stable.

But that didn't mean she had to look at all of life that way...even if she did at times.

"I appreciate everything you've done for me," she said. "Everything you tried to shield me from. I know I'm soft."

"You can't help the way you are," her father said. He was pacing and she hated it, but he'd lowered his voice.

"You make that sound like it's an insult."

"It's not meant to be. You're a beautiful person inside and out. Any man would be honored to be with you. But your emotions are always all over your face. You'd suck at poker and you know it."

"West likes that about me," she said. "I'm not like the people in his world."

"And that would bother you," her father said. "Be honest with me."

Abby sighed. She wouldn't lie to her father. "It does. I mean it did. But I met three of his siblings this weekend. Dad, they are just like Christian and his siblings together. It was funny to watch."

She'd always seen the Butlers as wealthy, but she didn't feel intimidated by them.

They had nothing compared to West.

"That doesn't change anything."

"Yes," she said. "It does. I don't have to work with him. I don't care how he is there."

"Don't give me that," her father said. "If a man is an asshole at his job, chances are he's an asshole in life too. You just don't see it."

She hated to think that. She worked with plenty of them too but tried to look at it from the other point of view. That maybe people had more going on in their lives she didn't know about.

"I don't need to see it because I don't believe it. Every single one of his siblings works for him or he bought them a business that falls under him. I heard it a few times from Braylon, Laken and Foster. No one gets a free ride. Everyone works, even his siblings."

"Because he could be a tyrant."

"No," she said, shaking her head. "He's not. I think people are afraid of him just like I'm afraid of the CEO at my job. He holds a power over me that I'd never have. That's human nature. But that doesn't mean the guy is a jerk."

"I've done a lot of work for wealthy people in my life," her father said. "And they can shit on you and then walk away with the last sheet of toilet paper without a thought of the rash you might get."

She grinned. It was not the first time her father had used words like that. Just never around her.

"You're right, that happens, but you don't know if it doesn't happen. I don't understand why you are acting this way. You were all cozy with Christian when Liz started to date him again. Going behind Liz's back and asking Christian to help you with her kitchen knowing she'd be ticked."

Her father turned away from her trying to hide his blush.

"That's different."

"How is it different? Because you know Christian and his family?"

"That's right. If I didn't know him, I'd treat him the same as I am this guy. I saw one daughter take off with a man I didn't get to know and I'll be damned if another one will fall into that situation."

Oh man. It never occurred to her that her father would feel he was responsible for Liz's abusive marriage.

She should have realized it though.

Her father shouldered the guilt for their mother's behavior and blamed himself for not being able to help his wife and keep their family together.

"West isn't Tanner. Liz and Christian met West a few days ago when he flew here to talk to me."

She told her father the whole situation. How she was upset when she found out who he was. That he continued to pursue her and get her to give him a chance.

"I don't like that your sister kept this from me and I'll be talking to her too. But the fact he's trying to win you over makes me think he's got control over you. You told him no and he didn't give up."

She frowned. She didn't want to think that.

No, she wouldn't.

"It's not the same. I feel something for him. If I didn't and I said no, I think he'd move on."

It was only that West wanted to prove she felt for him the same as he did for her.

Hiding her emotions had never been easy.

She'd always been the one to wear her heart on her sleeve, just as her father said. No poker face.

"I get the feeling he's someone that isn't used to being told no."

She didn't like that that had been brought up this weekend either.

But West's family *did* tell him no.

"I talked to his flight attendant on the way there. She had nothing but great things to say about West."

"She could have been told to say those things."

Abby didn't believe that. She felt she was a good judge of character and Susie said positive things about West, but also a few flaws.

That he worked too hard.

He never let his guard down.

It was hard for him to get close to anyone.

She supposed in his position, she could understand that.

"I don't think so," she said. "I think West is lonely and he won't tell anyone that or admit it."

"I doubt a billionaire could ever be lonely," her father said, snorting.

"Dad," she said. "You know I love you and respect you and always listen to you. But I think you're wrong. I think when you have that kind of money you're very lonely because you're always wondering if the people who are around you have motives."

Her father was quiet for a second. "Maybe he thinks you do."

She laughed. "No. I worried about that. He paid for everything in Aruba and I got mad a few times. I finally ended up buying us ice cream one day and he was annoyed over that. I told him to get over it."

"Ice cream," her father said. "He couldn't even let you buy that? That means he's a control freak."

"No," she said, trying not to get frustrated. "He's not. I told you, his father died when he was eighteen and he's the oldest of eight kids. He helped his mother raise them and if there was structure it was because it was the only way things got done. But he went to college shortly after too and had multiple jobs. He was working, he was in school, he was trying to be the man of the house with it. That's a lot on someone's shoulders who was still technically a kid in many ways. I don't think he's ever put himself first. Sounds like some other man I know and am looking at."

Her father wrinkled his nose when she made that bold statement.

"Not the same thing."

"Totally the same thing. You've always taught me not to judge people and you're doing it right now based on how much money he has. Don't you trust me enough to know how I feel? You know as well as I do I'd never be swayed by wealth. I saw what Liz went through. I saw and knew it for years even when you didn't."

"And you never said a word to me," her father snapped. "As if neither of you trusted me to handle it."

This was going south faster than West's jet flew.

"Dad, I'm not telling you I love him. I've known him for two weeks. I like and respect him. We are trying to learn more about each other in the next few weeks. I'm not stupid. I'm not going to set myself up to be hurt. If in a few weeks, things aren't working out, then I'll move on. I don't expect to have him drop everything and talk to me daily or see me multiple times a week. I don't want that and I know he doesn't either. But I don't want to be ignored and forgotten for days at a time."

She knew it was going to be a hard balance on a very thin wire, but if West thought this could work, then he'd have to prove it.

Going two days or so without much communication but a simple text would be fine. She'd understand. More so if seeing him on the weekend he was all in when they were together.

But if they went days like she didn't exist, then he tried

to buy her affection for one or two days, it wasn't going to work.

She didn't think she was a clingy person.

Never that.

But she knew what it was like to be pushed aside and ignored by someone you cared for.

She wouldn't let herself be put in that position again.

"If I find out that is happening, he's going to be having words with me," her father said.

She smiled and walked over to hug him. "I know you'll do it too. Please, talk to Liz. She'll reassure you."

"I'm going to be calling her the minute you leave."

She laughed. "Because you don't want me to know how upset you are with my actions. I understand."

"See," her father said. "You're still so sensitive."

"I am," she said. "It's my burden to carry and work around it. Not yours to shield me. If you want to call Liz while I'm here, do it."

"No," her father said. "I'll feel as if I can't say what I want because I don't want to hurt you. We both need to be apart for me to make the call."

She sighed. "I understand. See, I'm not being selfish. I understand your needs and hope that you will understand mine."

She kissed him on the cheek and drove home.

She had laundry to do and hoped the laundry room wasn't full with everyone else trying to get things done on the weekend.

If she was going to be busy the next few weekends she needed to rearrange her life during the week.

She could do it.

She just hoped West could too.

20

HARDEST CONVERSATION

"West," his mother said. "This is a surprise. I never get to see you this often. Are you still annoyed with me that I tricked you into going on vacation?"

"No," he said. He couldn't be annoyed now when she managed to open his eyes to so much he was doing wrong and missing out on in life.

"Then you're here to give Talia a hard time?"

"She's not even here," he said. "She's in college and she texted me the other day to thank me for the necklace I sent her."

His sister was picking on him about how nice it'd be to have a boutique on a tropical island.

Sorry, that wasn't the type of business he was investing in for her.

She had too much potential to just do that with her life.

Nor did he think Talia would be happy.

She loved jewelry and fashion. There would be an opportunity for her when she was ready and had a solid reasonable plan.

"She did love it," his mother said. "Just as much as I loved the scarf and hat you sent me. Thank you again."

His mother loved to garden. She'd spend hours outside weeding and planting. She liked having fashionable hats that she could wear while doing it.

"You're welcome," he said.

He remembered the shopping day with Abby and the fun the two of them had. He had more to shop for than she did. Most of his was rum for his brothers. They enjoyed that. Laken got jewelry too. His sister did like to accessorize.

"So tell me why you're here," his mother said. "You're normally last minute, but I feel you've got something on your mind."

He'd called her this morning and said he was traveling and would be close by and he'd like to stop.

"I wanted to tell you in person before it got back to you that I met someone."

His mother frowned. "What did you do?"

"Nothing," he argued.

"Then how could it get back to me if you didn't do something wrong?"

He didn't think of it that way. "Braylon, Laken and Foster met her this weekend in the Hamptons."

"You introduced a woman to some of your siblings? And you brought her to your oasis that only family goes to?"

It was the shocked look on his mother's face that told him this was going to be the hardest conversation.

His mother knew him the best. She understood right away.

"Yes, I did."

"How long have you been dating her for you to do that? And what is her name?"

"Her name is Abby Sherman. I met her in Aruba."

He didn't expect his mother to start laughing. Laughing so hard she was almost bent over with it.

"Seriously?" his mother said.

"I'm being serious," he said.

His mother stopped laughing. Then she smiled. "Now you sound like your father and me."

"Huh?" he asked.

"Your father was in the service on leave. I met him and we clicked. A few weeks together and well...we got married. Good thing too because you came nine months later."

His jaw dropped. "I knew you guys married fast but not a few weeks. You said like six months."

"We lied. We didn't want you to think poorly of us. No kid wants to think of their parents hooking up fast."

"Urgh, Mom."

"See. You're getting all offended. But it's the truth. We had known each other a few weeks and he had to leave again. It's not like I could go with him. But if we were married I could. We could live on base together."

He shook his head. He'd had no clue about this.

"And then you got pregnant?" he asked.

"It's possible you were conceived before. As I said, just a few weeks that we knew each other. I knew right away your father was the one. No second thoughts at all about picking up my life and moving. But again, I was a virgin."

"Mom!" he said. He didn't want to hear these things.

"Get over yourself, West. Tell me more about Abby."

He explained most of what was going on. From how they met, to spending time together. That he didn't tell her what he did for a living, but gave enough information she could have found out easily.

"Sounds like she was as lost as you for that week there."

"Why do you say that?" he asked.

"Because most women do some kind of search on a man they just met. More so in a situation like that. You could have lied about your name or withheld any part of your life, but you all but laid it out for her."

He sighed. Again, his mother figured it out when no one else had. There was part of him that hoped Abby would have known who he was while they were there.

"I don't go around announcing to the world who I am. There was a big part of me that liked she only knew me as West, the guy there on a working vacation."

"It probably never occurred to her that you'd be who you are."

"No," he said. "It didn't. I also know she has trust issues so I expected her to look into me. It's her sister who did it when she returned home."

"So she had every intention of continuing a long-distance relationship?" his mother asked.

"She had her doubts it could work, but she was keeping an open mind. Then when she found out, she felt like a fool." He waved his hand. "We are past it. I convinced her to give it a chance."

"I can only imagine how you did that. Fast forward to this weekend and why she met some of your siblings."

"I met her sister and future brother-in-law. I thought it was only fair. I think she was unsure of things even more because when she did decide to look me up she didn't see me with any women."

"Did you tell her why?"

"I was honest. I said that I haven't had time to date in years. Or not seriously. Most women like to have more attention paid to them. That I even have been neglecting my family but my mother told me to cut the shit."

"You didn't say that," his mother said.

"I did," he said. He told Abby more about it on the flight to drop her off. Abby found it both sweet and funny.

"Good for you. There shouldn't be any secrets even though it seemed you started out that way."

"Not on purpose," he said. "Though I felt something for her quickly, the other part of me wasn't sure enough that she might not go home and try something."

Like blackmail him though the chances of that were slim.

Though deep down he'd wanted her to know who he was, he still thought it was best she found out after.

It seemed to be working out now and they were over the first hump in his eyes.

"There is always that fear," his mother said.

"I don't see it. Laken liked her. Said she was down to earth. I think Laken was just happy to see me cooking and cleaning up in the kitchen."

"I don't know if anyone has seen you cook or clean in years."

"I clean at the holidays," he argued.

They still all got together for major holidays and his mother insisted on cooking, but everyone had to help out cleaning. Those were the rules.

"Because I tell you to," his mother said.

"I still do it."

"You do. Call Abby now," his mother said. "I want to make sure you aren't pulling one over on me."

"Why would you think that?" he asked.

"To get even with me for what Talia and I did."

"Mom, I don't play games like that."

"No, you're right. But I still want you to call her. Let's see if she picks up right away."

He frowned. "What does that mean?"

"Just do it," his mother said. "And how long are you staying? Do you want me to make dinner or not? You said you were on the way close by."

"Sort of," he said. "I wanted to tell you in person and flew to Albany with Abby. It was only a few more hours to get here. Since I was on the plane, I worked, so it's not any different than if I was working at home."

"Sure, it's different," his mother said. "But you didn't tell me if you were staying for dinner or if you wanted something to eat."

He looked at his watch. It was two. "I can stay for another hour if you want to cook something light or quick."

"I'll go light the grill. I've got a steak in the fridge. I know how you love your beef. I can throw together some home fries like you loved as a kid."

"That works," he said.

"Now call Abby before I start."

There was no getting out of this. He pulled his phone out and dialed, but it only rang and went to voicemail.

Rather than leave her a message, he sent her a text saying it was no big deal, that his mother wanted him to call just as he knew she would.

"Happy?" he said. "She must be busy."

She hadn't said what she was doing today, but he thought she'd be home by now. She'd texted that things went okay with her father.

He wasn't sure what that meant, but she would tell him when they talked next.

He could appreciate that she wasn't going to be someone who wanted long conversations in a text. Nothing annoyed him more.

Twenty minutes later, he was in the kitchen with his

mother having a beer while she was checking on the home fries in the oven.

His phone buzzed and he saw it was Abby.

"Hello," he said.

"Hi," she said. "Sorry. I was in the basement changing over my laundry and folding it. Then I put some away and didn't know my phone rang. I just saw your message."

"Put her on speaker," his mother said.

"Don't judge me on this conversation," he said, laughing. "My mother wants you on speaker."

He hit the button. "Hi, Abby. I'm Aileen Carlisle. I just wanted to know if you existed."

Abby laughed. "I do exist. I sort of thought the same thing when I found out about your son."

"Oh, he's real," his mother said. "All nine pounds and two ounces of him I pushed out."

"Mom!" he said, mortified. He'd never known her to be this way.

Of course it's not like he brought women home to introduce them to his mother either.

He might never do it again.

"It's fine," Abby said. "I was a tiny baby. My mother said it all the time. Grosses me out when she says I just slipped out. My father insisted he wanted to push the nurse out of the way to catch me. He says he's been catching me ever since."

His mother got this soft emotional look on her face and whispered, "Awwww."

"I think you are doing a good job landing on your feet now," he said.

"I think so, but who knows?" she said.

"I won't keep you," he said. "I know you've got things to do."

"West is trying to get you off the phone because he's afraid I'm going to embarrass him," his mother said.

"Like you're doing right now," he said, snorting.

"It's fine," Abby said. "We all have family members who like to embarrass us."

"My mother is feeding me dinner before I get back on the plane. Can I call you in an hour or so or are you busy?"

"I'll be around," she said. "Give me a call when you can."

He hung up after that and turned to his mother. "I like her," she said.

"From that five minute call?"

"Yep. She didn't jump when you called. It's not like she carries her phone with her everywhere since she didn't even know she had a message. And she told you to call her when you could. I bet she doesn't hold you to the hour either."

"No," he said. "She won't."

"She's going to keep you on your toes. This is going to be fun to see."

"Gee," he said. "Thanks for that."

"It's what a mother does."

21

GOOD SOLUTION

"Okay, well this is exactly what I thought it'd look like," Abby said two weeks later. Last week she had a repeat of the first weekend in the Hamptons minus his siblings.

It was a lot and a long day to fly there after work, then the helicopter ride to his weekend house.

This weekend, he decided to have them go to his penthouse.

They were on the fifteenth floor. Normally he had a driver bring him home from the airport, but they took the helicopter here because he said it was faster and he didn't want to give up one minute with her.

He wasn't waiting for her at the airport this time either. She flew by herself, but he was on the roof when she landed.

She wasn't sure what she would have done if he wasn't here.

Now they were inside and this was the wealth and class she'd been expecting when she found out who he really was.

It almost seemed cold.

"That doesn't sound positive," he said.

"It's so different than your house," she said. "The one in the Hamptons." She had to clarify that, as he'd told her he had a few more properties in the US too. He said he'd take her to them another time. She just shrugged.

Only one more weekend of this and they'd be at their thirty days.

As much as she was looking forward to seeing him and missing him during the week, it was tiring. And wearing on her already.

Though he was attentive when they were together, she knew he snuck away to deal with calls and texts and she let it go.

"It is," he said. "I don't spend a lot of time here other than sleeping or working. I had someone come in and decorate and though I didn't have a problem with it, it's not welcoming."

"It's not horrible," she said. "It's just you can tell a bachelor lives here."

Everything was dark and polished. Shiny even.

"Sorry about that," he said. "I figured you'd like the other house better and I was right."

"It's not where I have to live," she said, laughing. "Nor could I."

He looked at her and nodded his head but didn't say anything else. She didn't expect he would.

She didn't want to be mean, but she didn't see herself being here long term. No way.

The Hamptons, she could do it. She'd be bored and have to find a job for sure, but she could live in that house.

Though she wasn't sure why she was even letting her mind think that after three weeks.

It was just fleeting thoughts that popped up now and again during the week when they didn't talk much.

They texted daily and she was slightly shocked over that.

Even if it was only an early morning or late night text. He almost always reached out to her first. She started to feel guilty about that, but she knew he was busy.

He'd told her the other day he appreciated that she wasn't needy.

She laughed over that comment. There had been times in her life she felt she was.

"I understand," he said. "Can I shower before we get dinner?"

"Do you want me to cook?" she asked.

"Nope. I'm going to take you out. In the city, that is the thing to do. You should at least see both sides of how I live."

"I figured."

"Give it a chance," he said. "I'm only here during the week, but I thought you should see this too."

"I know. Sorry. I shouldn't be this way. There are so many people who would love it. It's just not me."

"It takes getting used to," he said.

"I'll take your word for it."

She yawned and he came over to hug her. "Tired?"

"Yeah," she said. "It feels nonstop lately."

It was as close as she was going to get to complaining. They said thirty days and one more weekend wouldn't be the end of the world and then they'd have a talk and figure it out. She just couldn't do this every weekend and he'd have to understand that.

It's not how she lived her life. It's not like she had a lot of friends she went out and did things with, but a few had asked her to go out this weekend and she had to make up some excuse because she didn't want anyone to know about

West or the fact that she was flying in and out on the weekends.

"It's getting to you, isn't it?"

No reason to lie. "Long days," she said. "I'm not used to it like you."

"And when you land it's still a lot of travel to get to me," he said.

"Yes," she said.

"How about I come to you next weekend?"

"Really?" she asked. Her father had been asking to meet West. She'd told him how the conversation went with her father but not much more.

"Yes," he said. "Though would you be offended if I said that I don't think I can comfortably sleep in your bed for two nights?"

"No," she said. "I know it's small. What do you want to do?"

"Would you mind staying in a hotel?" he asked. "It's probably asking a lot when you live there."

"I can do that," she said. "I suppose I can upgrade my bed if I need to."

He grinned. "That means this will go on for more than thirty days?"

"I thought we'd talk about that more next weekend. But the fact that you're willing to come to me helps."

"I know," he said. "It's selfish of me."

"I get it," she said. "I don't live like this. It's what you're used to."

There wasn't anything she could do about it either. Even if she wanted to get a nicer apartment, it'd be tight money-wise and why would she do that to herself when nothing was guaranteed with her and West?

On top of that, an upgrade still wouldn't be anything *he'd* be used to.

"Don't do that or think it," he said. "Let's just work with the fact that you're willing to go past the thirty days. But you can say it, the every weekend of you flying isn't going to work."

"It won't," she said. "Plus I've got friends too. And I'm sure you've got things to do on the weekends other than spending it with me."

"We'll figure it out," he said. "I'm sure we can come up with a good solution."

She liked that he was being reasonable about this.

That he wasn't trying to control it or her like her father worried.

He didn't ask her how it would work or her thoughts, but maybe that would come later on.

"Next weekend, do you think you could meet my father? Maybe have dinner with him and Liz and Christian?"

They were in his bedroom where she'd followed him and put her clothes away while he was unbuttoning his shirt so he could take a shower.

"I'd love to," he said. "Is your father okay with that? Is he ready?"

She moved over and hugged him. "More than ready. I think he needs to meet you."

"Why haven't you said anything before now?" he asked.

She was staring at his chest. He was unbuttoning his pants and dropping them down now.

"Huh?"

He laughed. "I asked why you haven't said anything before. Do you want to get in the shower with me?"

"I'm hungry," she said. "Are you going to distract me so that we are in there for a long time?"

"Maybe," he said. "But there is a restaurant not that far from here we can walk to."

She wasn't sure how she felt about going out in public with him before the thirty days, but since they just agreed to work it out, there was no reason to say no.

She wanted to continue and to do that; they had to try.

She pulled her shirt over her head and started to undress with him and followed him into the bathroom.

No time or need to wash her hair, but his hands were working her up as they washed her and then helped rinse her off.

All he did was tease and leave her on edge.

"I cry no fair," she said.

He smirked. "I'll make it up to you later."

"How do I have to dress for this restaurant?" she asked.

"Casual. I'm putting on jeans and a T-shirt."

"Oh," she said. "Thanks for that."

"Don't thank me. It's a pub. Could be I've got some ownership of it. Best to tell you that now. We'll get a place in the back out of the way if you want."

She let out a breath. "Thanks. Can I let you know when we get there? I mean I shouldn't always want to hide unless you want to. And if you do, that is fine too."

"I'm leaving it up to you."

That let her know he was more invested than maybe she was.

There was a lot of guilt over that, but she couldn't change the fact that a few weeks in didn't mean she was ready for her whole world to change.

22

GOOD ADVICE

Somehow West and Abby made it the thirty days. Or close enough.

He knew she was struggling and hated that she didn't once tell him that.

Nothing more than it was tiring. He still wondered if he didn't ask her if she would have admitted it, but he was thrilled that she had.

His mother had told him weeks ago and then more recently that a relationship was give and take and just because he had the wallet didn't me he had the only voice.

Good advice to have.

"I know it was silly sleeping at the hotel last night," he said.

"We could have slept on the plane if it stayed in Albany," she said.

"You should have said something," he said. "I could have arranged that."

"No," she said. "Talk about wasteful."

He laughed. "It stays at JFK. It's not like I've got a private place at my house for it."

"I didn't think about it. Doesn't matter. The hotel is fine. My father is cooking and he can't wait to meet you. I'm glad I got to show you a little bit of my area too."

They'd gone to a small town called Lake George. There were quaint shops up and down they walked in and out of and got on a steamboat for a cruise around the lake.

Abby had laughed and said she hadn't done this since she was a kid and wasn't even sure what made her suggest it.

He knew it had more to do with the fact she wanted him to see what her life was like growing up.

He reminded her that his wasn't that much different. In some cases, he had less.

One income and a lot more mouths to feed.

He knew it was hard for her to see that now.

"Do I have to worry about being grilled?" he asked.

"You can handle it," she said. "I know you'll be respectful. My father just doesn't want to be looked down on."

"Never," he said seriously. "I don't want him to feel that way either."

His mother had drilled that into his head too. That to think of the father he lost and how he'd feel if the roles were reversed and Abby were one of his sisters.

They pulled up to the house she grew up in.

"It's not that big, but Liz and I had our own rooms."

"It's better than some of the places I lived in. I always had to share a room."

"I don't know that I could handle having that many siblings."

"It has its moments," he said. "We haven't all been together since Christmas. Normally Christmas and Thanksgiving are the two everyone tries for."

"Not birthdays because there are too many of them?" she asked.

"That's it. Some of the siblings see the other. I do make sure my mother is where she wants to be. She won't let me send the jet for her though."

"I don't think I'd like that either."

His mother lectured him about being wasteful, but he brushed it off. He just wanted his mother and his family comfortable.

He shut his rental off and got out. "Is Liz here already?"

There were two trucks in the driveway so he was assuming one was Christian's. The other said Sherman Fencing on it.

"Yep," she said. "They knew we had plans today."

"I hate not bringing anything," he said.

"Don't worry about it. We've got beer and didn't need that. You might need one though."

West smiled. He wasn't sure why he was so nervous other than the fact that in this short time he knew beyond a doubt he was falling in love with Abby and didn't want to do anything to ruin it. If that meant having to give her some space, he'd do it.

His parents had loved long and strong with a lot of time apart.

It's just he didn't think he'd be someone who could do that.

Nor would he. A few weeks was one thing.

Until he could convince her to move closer.

He had it all worked out in his head.

She could live in the Hamptons and he could commute back and forth easily enough and split his time. Three to four days at each place giving them enough time apart and together.

When the time was right, he'd tell her the plan.

Abby opened the door and he walked in behind her. "Hi,

Dad. This is West." Trevor Sherman was standing there waiting, his arms crossed and a stern look on his face. Nothing like the kind friendly father Abby had bragged about for weeks.

The one that put her and Liz first all the time.

Though he supposed it all went hand in hand.

"Nice to meet you," West said, reaching his hand forward. Both of them had the same firm handshake.

"The same," Trevor said. He knew it was forced, but the man was going to put on a good front for his daughter.

"Be nice, Dad," Abby said. "Things are going well and you know it."

"So it seems," Trevor said. "Come on in. I've got burgers made and Liz put together a few salads. I heard you liked burgers."

He grinned. "I do."

Liz took the beer out of his hand. "I'll pour a few of these and you can go sit on the deck with Christian."

He nodded and followed Christian out while the girls stayed in the kitchen with their father.

"Trevor is the best there is," Christian said. "But they've all had a hard life."

"I've heard some of it."

"About Liz?" Christian asked.

"Yes."

Abby had explained about her sister's previous marriage and that Trevor blamed himself.

"Trevor is only doing what he felt he should have done for Liz. He'll be fine. In the end, he only wants what is best for his girls."

"That's all that I want too," he said.

"Then it all should be good," Christian said.

He was halfway through his beer when Trevor decided

to get personal. "Tell me your intentions with Abby. You live hours away, she is here. She can't be traveling and flying everywhere each weekend on your whim. She has a job and family and friends here."

"Dad," Abby said. "I told you we have no plans just yet."

"We'll work it out the best for Abby," he said. "I'm not someone that likes to be away from someone I care about for months at a time. Even weeks. But I know things happen. I don't have a problem coming here if it's too much for Abby to always come to me."

"My place isn't that big," she said. "I know that."

"It's fine," he said. "We'll figure it out together."

That answer seemed to satisfy Trevor, but West noticed Abby was frowning. Maybe he should have let her talk some more, but she didn't.

"How come at your age you've never been married or in a serious relationship?"

"You're getting personal, Dad," Liz said.

"I have a right to do that. I should have done it with you and didn't."

"It's okay," he said. "I've put my career first and that was wrong of me. Life got away from me while I was trying to set my family up along with it. Maybe it's time for me to put myself first."

Abby smiled when he said that. At least the frown was gone and he was only telling the truth.

"Can we stop with those questions now, Dad?" Abby asked.

"Sure," Trevor said. "I need to get the burgers on the grill anyway. Do you follow any sports, West?"

"I'm finalizing majority shares in the New York Hawks if you like hockey. I could get you some good seats."

Her father laughed. "I played hockey as a kid."

"I didn't know that, Dad," Abby said.

"Guess we don't know everything about everyone, do we?" Trevor asked, but he was looking at West when he said that.

23

TAKEN CARE OF WELL

F ive weeks later, Laken walked into West's office ten minutes before their scheduled meeting.

"You're early," he said. He kept to his schedule for a reason. He was stretched thin.

"I'm allowed to be early as your sister. I waited as long as I could."

"What's going on?" he asked, leaning back in his chair.

Laken moved over to the leather couch in the seating area to the right and sat.

Guess it was going to be an informal meeting.

He got up and joined her, sitting across in the matching chair.

"Mom just called."

"Okay," he said. "Nothing odd there."

"She wants us all together in July. For the Fourth."

"That's during the week," he said. This was all news to him. "And we only get together for Thanksgiving and Christmas."

"She said the weekend after," Laken said. "She wants to meet Abby."

He let out a sigh. He'd expected this but not to have the whole family together.

Talk about throwing his girlfriend of two months to the wolves.

They'd made it the thirty days and then another. He was thrilled.

Did they see each other weekly? No. As much as he wanted to, it wasn't working.

It was too much to ask her to fly here weekly and he couldn't always swing it to see her. It'd been two weekends since they'd had time together and she was flying to his house in the Hamptons Friday morning. She'd taken the day off and he was going to try to get out early so they could have a long weekend together.

He did stop to surprise her ten days ago. Actually, he was on his way back from another trip and told the pilot to stop in Albany for a few hours.

He and Abby went to dinner, they went back to her place and squeezed into her tiny double bed, then he returned to his jet and flew home.

He didn't know how people did this long-distance thing successfully without having the means he did.

Not his problem.

His problem was figuring out what was going on with his mother.

"She's met Abby," he said. "She's talked to her twice via video."

Twice his mother called when he was with Abby and wanted her on the screen to "meet" her.

"That's not the same thing in Mom's mind," Laken argued. "I just got an earful on how this is the first girlfriend you've had that she can remember."

"That she's known about," he said.

"Come on now," Laken argued. "For the past decade or more those were bedmates, not girlfriends."

"Whatever," he said. No use denying it.

"Mom is going to call you next. I should get a bonus for giving you a heads up," Laken said, grinning.

"You get a bonus with every new business I acquire and you set up," he said, laughing.

His sister and Braylon were needed more than most in his businesses. He made sure they were taken care of well.

"This is a family bonus," she said. "You need to deal with Talia too."

He let out a sigh. "Is she being a pain to you?"

"I know I'm her only sister. I get it. But our age gap and outlook on life make it hard for me to even have a reasonable conversation with her."

"What's going on? She told me she needed time to figure things out. No reason to push her into something if she's not ready."

His youngest sister had to be handled differently, he knew.

"That's the problem, West. We've all treated her like a baby. Mom too. No one pushes her like we were pushed. She thinks that is the norm. The rest of us finished college and were ready to dive into life and our careers. To prove to you we had what you were looking for and wanted to be part of your team."

He sighed. "I didn't want you guys to do it for that reason."

"I don't know about anyone else," Laken said. "But for me, I needed to be a part of this. So did Braylon. Foster too but in his own way. The rest of them are part of it in their own way too. Nelson wants to be here with you."

"He's not ready," he said.

"I know. He doesn't see it though. What he sees is that you were doing it at his age and why can't he?"

"I earned it at his age. He is having the opportunity handpicked for him. He can't see the difference and he's going to have to before he can get in this office."

He'd had Nelson at two different companies that he owned working under other CEOs. Smaller companies. Getting experience and running divisions.

So far it wasn't working because there were those CEOs who felt they were being watched and forced to babysit even if Nelson wasn't causing issues.

Nelson had a chip on his shoulder that needed to be knocked off though. Being his younger brother wasn't always a good thing and those trying to mentor him were guarded.

"That's the thing. I think he needs to be shoved down a few pegs," Laken said, laughing.

He grinned. "So I'm not the only one that thinks he feels he's entitled?"

"Nope," Laken said. "It's this generation. I can't help it. Put him here in a lower level management position on that income. I'm sure what you're paying him in another state wouldn't get him much more than a loft to rent here. Let him know what it's like to come in and *work*."

"He'll be pissed," he said, laughing.

"Let him be pissed," Laken said. "Maybe he'll work a little harder to prove he has what it takes and not just want to be next to you because you invited him."

"I'll think about it," he said. "Back to Mom. Foster will never go. You can barely get him to leave Long Island. I'm lucky he came out to meet Abby in the Hamptons."

"Foster will go if Rowan does," she said.

He laughed. "Then we won't all be together," he said.

"Because you can't get Rowan away from Long Beach. He loves the distance and life he's got away from everyone."

Of all his brothers, Rowan was the most carefree laid back one. He knew what he wanted right away and it wasn't to sit in an office, but his brother was smart.

He had what it took because he had a vision and a creative mind.

Rowan's degree in digital art from UCLA and his time surfing just reinforced what he was meant to do. Surf shaping, he'd learned it was called years ago. As long as his brother was happy, so he was.

"He does," Laken said. "But Mom has already reached out to him. She told me she's talked to everyone but you and Braylon."

"Oh boy, she's making her way through us in reverse order."

That was her meaning business.

If she needed his help, she came to him first.

This meant she was getting everyone on her side and it would leave him no choice, being outnumbered.

"That looks it," Laken said.

He turned his head when his office door opened. No one came in but his assistant when he was in a meeting unless the building was on fire or something else was blowing up.

It was Braylon with a red face.

"Mom?" he asked, letting out a sigh.

"Sorry, West. I just got a pretty severe lecture about having no life and I should take a page from your book and need to spend more time with you. You know we don't like to hang up on Mom when she gets on a roll. I could only shut her up by agreeing to go home in a few weeks."

"All she had to do was ask me," he said.

Both Braylon and Laken started to laugh. "That never

works," Laken said. "That's how you ended up meeting Abby. She guilted you into it by using the rest of us."

"Mom didn't lie about how everyone was feeling about me though, right? Don't lie. I saw it and ignored it."

"No," Braylon said. "She didn't. We should have talked to you about it ourselves."

"I wouldn't have heard," he said. It was in the past and he was trying to do a better job at being a brother rather than everyone's boss.

"Get your ears open now," Braylon said. "Mom will be calling you later. And sorry for the interruption. Just wanted to give you a heads up, but it looks as if Laken already did."

"No one else felt the need to," he said.

"They were earlier in on Mom's calls. Once it gets to Laken you're outnumbered."

His mother was dirty that way. He liked to think he got some of his shrewd business sense from her.

"It's fine," he said. "I'll talk to Abby. I'm sure she'll be okay with it. I'm going to assume you guys will fly there with me?"

"Yeah," Laken said. "But I've got to be in Utah on that Monday, so I'd like to come home early on Sunday if possible."

"Not a big deal," he said. "I'm sure Abby is working. She doesn't have a lot of time to take and she took this Friday off to come see me. We are spending a long weekend in the Hamptons."

"Why don't you go there Thursday night," Laken said. "And work from home there. You haven't seen Abby as much, she might appreciate you being there instead of her sitting around waiting for you."

"I'll think about it," he said. He didn't need his single siblings telling him how to manage his relationship.

Braylon left his office and he and Laken got back to work.

He tried to focus on what needed to be done, but all he could think of was Abby and he was wondering if that was part of the problem.

He'd never been someone that couldn't put his career first. It seemed for years he even put that before his family more than he should have.

Now, he wanted Abby first but was terrified she didn't want the same thing and was trying not to upset their dynamic.

He hoped bringing her to meet the whole family at once didn't cause an issue. He knew he'd never pick a woman over his family, but for once, he was torn that he might be forced to do that if Abby wasn't willing to meet his mother and other siblings in person.

24

PART OF SOMETHING

"Are you going to tell Mom about West?" Liz asked her two days later. Abby and her sister were going to dinner with their mother. They were driving the twenty-five minutes to Clifton Park where her mother was in a supportive housing facility. She'd been there for over six months and was doing well.

"I want to," she said. "I mean it would make her feel like she's part of the family again, right?"

"I don't want to tell you what to do," Liz said. "But be careful. It hasn't been that long and Mom is an addict."

"She's recovering," she argued.

"She's still an addict. She sure the hell doesn't need to know anything about West. Not when she could tell someone she lives with."

Abby sighed. "I know. I thought of that too. I guess there was just a part of me that wanted her to feel like she was part of something with us again."

"She has to earn that, Abby," Liz said firmly.

Her sister always could draw the line in the sand better

than her. Maybe because Liz was older and remembered more of what their mother did.

Abby just remembered that her mother left and made promises she never kept.

That she'd gotten her hopes up so much to have them dashed again and again.

All she ever wanted was a normal family and life. The one she dreamed of when she played with her Barbies and created that life in her head.

Her father did the best he could and she thought it was pretty great.

Not that she was happy with her father recently, but he was getting better.

West had been great to her father. Treated him like the father of his girlfriend and not like someone beneath him.

Not that she'd ever be with someone who was like that.

Since that visit, she hadn't flown to see West as much. She hoped he wasn't upset over it, but she just couldn't always drop everything in her life for him and she wouldn't do that for any man.

She knew his siblings found it funny and she believed that West was fine with it. It's not like he was sitting around waiting on her either.

The fact he surprised her one week for dinner on his way back home was awesome.

She'd been all giddy when his call came in and she was able to even answer it at work. Most times she didn't take personal calls at work, but since West hardly ever called her during the day, she knew it might be important.

He'd landed right when she was getting out of work, she went to the airport to get him, they went to dinner, back to her place, then she returned him to the airport. She was home by nine and it'd been worth the running around to spend a few hours with him.

She had to remind herself, he had it worse. He didn't get back to his penthouse until after eleven, she was sure. She didn't hear from him again until the next day. He was in the habit of texting her in the morning. Sometimes it woke her up, but she never complained. If she was in the shower, then she replied when she was out. They might not text again until later that night.

Again, sometimes she was in bed, but in her mind, he wasn't not communicating because he was afraid she wasn't around. She got back to him when she could, just like if she sent him a text midday he did the same thing. Replied when he could.

She didn't want to think of him as being distant, but rather busy. It might not be the relationship she'd always thought she'd have with a man she was falling in love with and she had to decide if she could accept that.

"It's hard for me to tell Mom she has to earn it," she said.

"No one says you have to be firm with her," Liz said. "Or say that. I'm just reminding you what we've been through and how much you want to tell Mom about West."

"I know," she said. "I understand. I think I'll just tell her I have a boyfriend. She knows I won that trip to Aruba but didn't ask that many questions. Just said that it sounded nice."

"That's right," Liz said. "Her life isn't all about family. She wants us in her life, but we aren't number one, and right now, we shouldn't be. Her focus has to be on getting healthy. Maybe being reminded of us isn't always good for her."

She started to sniffle. "That's mean."

Liz looked over from the road she was watching while she drove. "I don't mean it that way, Abby. I'm just saying that she's sick. It won't go away on its own or with a simple pill. We don't know what caused everything, but the truth is, she couldn't handle being a mother and a wife. She didn't want it."

"She didn't?" Abby asked.

Liz looked at her and then back to the road. "I'm sorry. I shouldn't have said that."

"Tell me. I don't know the things you do."

"I still shouldn't have said it," Liz said.

"Stop treating me like a baby. Dad did it for years too. If you want me to understand, then I need the truth."

"You're right. I told Dad that for years too. He didn't want you to have the memories I did. You're...softer than me."

"More emotional," she said. "You can tell me that."

Liz grinned. "Fine. You're more emotional. There were a lot of fights when you were younger. Mom said that she didn't want to be a mother. That she only had kids because of Dad."

She'd always felt that she was the cause of her mother's breakdown. She'd heard that her mother was fine before she was born.

"Dad would feel horrible hearing that," she said. "I just want to cry for him."

"Dad said it wasn't true. I believe him over Mom. He said that Mom wanted kids. It was always her idea and he was the one that worried having another child might be too hard for her, but it's what she wanted and I think he felt that maybe it would help ground her."

"So it was me?" she asked.

"Don't cry," Liz said. "It's not you. It's not your fault. Don't even think that. Dad and I love you. Mom does too. Dad would have done anything back then to get her better and she was so sure she wanted another child and he knew that he could step up and help. It just didn't work out the way anyone thought. But it's not you. It's something within Mom. And even then, she chose to self-medicate with drugs and alcohol. She could have stayed on her meds and been able to live a pretty complete life. *Never* think otherwise. She had a support system but decided to find another one."

It was hard for Abby not to think she was somewhat to blame for what happened in her mother's life.

"Did Mom drink and do drugs before me?" she asked. She had to know this.

"Yes," Liz admitted. "Dad wouldn't want you to know that, but it's true. That's why it's not you. She'd been in and out getting help and she'd stop on her own or she'd hide the fact she was doing drugs. She was clean when she was pregnant and I think Dad just felt so much hope."

"I guess I'm not the only one that was hurt by all of this," she said.

"No," Liz said. "We all lived it."

"You and Dad more. You tried to shield me just like Dad is trying to shield me from getting hurt with West."

"Dad will stop now. I talked to him. He's fine. He hasn't said anything negative about your relationship, has he?"

"No. Not since he met West. Nothing more than just to be careful. I hear that a lot."

"When you have kids someday you'll be saying that to them their whole life too."

"I'm sure you're right. Let's talk about something else. I don't want Mom to know I've been crying and we are almost there."

She pulled her purse out and fixed her makeup as best as she could. Thankfully she didn't wear much to begin with.

"You're going to see West tomorrow?" Liz asked.

"Yes. I took the day off. I haven't seen him in almost two weeks. He was here last week just for a few hours."

"Things are working out well with this?"

"They are," she said. "I mean I miss him, but I get it. I think if I lived in the same city as him I wouldn't see him any more during the week either. This way when we are together, he focuses on our time. That's better if you ask me."

"I think you're right. And you did the right thing saying it shouldn't be weekly. You've got friends and a life here and you shouldn't ever put your life on hold for a man."

Liz had done that with her first husband.

"I learned from you, but I'd never do it anyway. It's all good. I'm still a fish out of water when we are in Manhattan. But I love it in the Hamptons. Sometimes we go out to eat, but mainly we just spend the time together relaxing and talking and watching movies. We had a picnic on the beach once too. The weather is going to be nice this weekend so I hope to sit by the water and work on my tan again."

"Good for you," Liz said. "You deserve it."

"Just like you deserve Christian."

"Yes, I do," Liz said, laughing.

Ten minutes later they were pulling into the home their mother lived in. She came out the front door and jumped in Liz's car.

"Hi, Mom," she said. "You look nice."

Her mother had put some weight on in the past several months, her hair was washed and combed and she had on a pretty shirt that Liz had bought her when they'd taken her mother shopping for some clothes a few months ago.

"Thank you," her mother said. "These are the clothes you picked out. The shirt is so pretty."

"The peach color looks lovely on you," Abby said.

Her mother's hair was shoulder length now and Liz had brought her mom for a haircut a month ago. The gray was blended in with the shoulder-length cut that her mother could just wash and go and comb it. That was an improvement from other times.

"Thank you," her mother said. Her mother was smiling and her eyes were clear from what she could see. Another improvement, but Liz would be able to notice more than her.

They drove to a restaurant her mother had picked out and parked.

When they were seated inside and their drinks ordered, Liz started. "Christian and I decided to get married the Saturday after Thanksgiving. November thirtieth. We figured most families would be around for that holiday anyway."

"That's wonderful," her mother said. "I hope I'll be invited."

"Of course you will be," Liz said. "We'll take you dress shopping too. It's not going to be a big wedding. It's my second and though it's Christian's first, he doesn't want anything over the top."

Abby was going to be Liz's maid of honor for a second time, but she knew this one would stick.

She hadn't brought it up to West yet. It was too early to do that. She'd mentioned the date of the wedding and if they were still together, it would be assumed he'd be there.

It's not like all that many people knew she was dating someone, let alone dating West.

"That's wonderful," her mother said. "What's been going on in your life, Abby? You look to be losing some of your tan from your trip."

She looked at Liz. "I've got a boyfriend."

"What's his name?" her mother asked. Her mother seemed more attentive than normal too. "His name is West. He's great. A little older than me, but it's all good. Maybe I need that in my life."

Liz laughed and winked at her. "It's good to hear," her mother said and then just changed to another topic.

She tried not to be hurt that her mother didn't ask more about her life but then knew it was for the best. It'd keep her from withholding information about her boyfriend.

25

SURPRISE YOU

"What are you doing here?" Abby asked West as she boarded his jet the next day.

"I thought I'd surprise you," he said. "I could have asked Susie but thought you might have wanted to see me."

"I'm thrilled to see you," she said, giving a big hug.

He'd texted her last night to see if she'd be willing to get an early flight so they could spend more time together. He'd never said he was going to be on the plane with her because he didn't want to promise something he might not be able to do.

But when she'd said earlier was better, he'd asked his pilot to be ready to get Abby at six in the morning.

That meant he was up and at the airport by four thirty, but he didn't care.

He was going to take the time to be with her today, tomorrow and part of Sunday. The fact she was willing to take the day off of work for them gave him hope she'd be agreeable to meeting his mother in a few weeks.

"Good," he said. "I know it's early. Sorry about that."

"Don't be sorry. Are you working from home?"

"I've got a call at ten. We should be home at that point. I'll take the call and then the rest of your time is my time. Or my time is your time."

She smiled and gave him a big quick kiss. "No Susie at all?"

"No," he said. "Just me. And the pilots."

"So we can go lie down in your room for the flight home?"

He grinned. "We can."

"You're not even dressed up," she said. "No fantasy about seducing the boss."

She grabbed his hand and led him to the back while he took her bag from her. "I'm not your boss," he said. "Sometimes I think you're the boss of me."

She laughed. "I don't think anyone is your boss."

He wanted to ask if she was thinking of working for him. If she thought maybe she'd want to move closer.

No, she'd never ask that. Not when she didn't like him paying for everything as it was.

"My mother insists she still is," he said. Might as well put that out there.

"I think most parents feel that way. Do you have to check in with the pilots or anything? I shouldn't have dragged you back here. I just realized we've got to be seated and our seatbelts on to take off."

"I'll let him know we are ready," he said. "We can sit in the seats closest to the room. He'll flip the light off when we can get up."

"Do you think they'll know what we are doing?" she asked quietly.

"No," he said. "When Susie isn't here that is how we

communicate or he calls back to me. The phones will all answer and just ring over the speaker."

"Okay," she said, finding her seat and buckling in.

When West came walking out a few minutes later, he heard the engines and felt the plane moving. "He just got cleared for takeoff, so it was good timing."

He sat next to her, his long legs out in front. "How was your visit with your mother last night?"

"Good," she said. "I told her I was dating you."

"You did?" he asked. "What did you say?"

"Not much," she said quickly. "Just that I had a boyfriend and your name was West. Liz had already warned me not to say more. My mother is and will always be an addict. I know that. I can't forget it. Plus she lives with people we don't know or trust. We don't know what she could say to them. In the end she didn't even ask how we met or anything about you at all."

He felt bad about that. He could tell by the tone of her voice that though she wouldn't have told her mother much, she might have wanted at least some interest expressed. She'd said before how she'd played with dolls and made up a life as a child and he wondered if at times she still thought that was what she wanted and wasn't getting it with their relationship.

Though she never once voiced that.

Maybe it was a good time to bring up the visit to North Carolina.

"Speaking of mothers...mine would like to meet you."

"She met me a few weeks ago on video," she said.

"In person," he said. "The weekend after July Fourth. She wants all the siblings home to meet you."

"Oh," she said. "Can you do it?"

"You don't have a problem with it?"

"No," she said. "Unless you don't want me to go."

"I want you to go," he said. "If you couldn't I'd probably get grounded."

She laughed. "Not sure that is possible. I bet you weren't ever grounded as a kid."

"You'd be surprised," he said.

He and Braylon used to get into it the most. Then they'd gang up on Laken.

He supposed it was all coming back to him now.

"Just let me know the plans. I'm going to assume we'll leave from your house?"

"We'll leave from Manhattan most likely. Braylon, Laken and Foster will fly with us. Foster isn't happy he has to come to the city, but he doesn't have a choice unless he wants to book his own flight and sit with other people."

His brother would never do that for a quick trip home.

He'd suck up the drive into the city to have a quick quiet flight.

"Then I should get there on Friday like normal and then fly out Saturday?" she asked.

"I think that will be the plan, but I'll let you know as we get closer. Thank you."

She put her hand on his thigh. "Don't thank me for that," she said. She let out a little giggle.

He wasn't used to seeing this side of her.

Correct. He hadn't seen it since they'd met in Aruba.

He'd had this fear she'd be upset after the dinner with her mother but was glad it didn't work out that way.

The plane was lifting now and he felt his dick shifting in his pants. He knew the minute the light went off, Abby was going to rush him to the back.

Or maybe that was his hope.

"What will I get to thank you for?" he asked.

"You're going to find out," she said.

When he felt the plane start to level out, he waited for the light. It went off and they both got up and moved quickly behind the door to his room.

He turned the lock but didn't need to. It's not like he expected anyone to come in.

"Get undressed," she said. "We don't have much time before we have to get back in our seats."

He pulled his T-shirt over his head. He hadn't bothered to do much more than put on jeans with it and sneakers. No reason to dress up and every reason to be comfortable.

"You have to do the same," he said. "Have you been thinking about becoming a member of the mile high club? Is that what this was about?"

He wouldn't lie and say he'd never had sex back here, but it wasn't often.

At least Abby hadn't asked him.

"No," she said. "Well, kind of, but it's more about having fun. You know, feeling as if you have to rush. Plus I've got a surprise for you."

"I'm getting one now," he said. She wiggled out of her shorts and was all but diving onto his bed.

He kicked his jeans away and joined her, his mouth going to hers, his arms around her back, pushing her naked breasts against his chest.

"What surprise is that?"

"I got a birth control shot in my arm last month. We are good without condoms if you want. If not, I understand. I mean don't think I do this often. I don't. You're actually only the second person I haven't worn a condom with and the first was a few years ago."

He hadn't heard about that or why. Had to be someone

she was serious about. She'd never said anything and he realized he'd never asked.

He didn't want to get jealous and told himself not to.

He had her now, not that faceless man.

"I'm good with it," he said. "Not something I've done before."

"Ever?" she asked, leaning back.

"No," he said. "You know I haven't dated anyone seriously."

She didn't look as if she believed him. "But you've dated. And it's only been a few months for us."

"Enough time for me to know the difference," he said softly.

"Difference?" she asked.

She said she wanted to give him a surprise, but maybe it was time he gave her one.

He rolled fast, got on top of her, locked their hands together and put them over her head.

His mouth went to hers kissing her softly.

A few pecks here and there, her legs moving apart, him dropping between them, then finding his way deep inside.

"The difference is what I feel for you," he said. "What I've been feeling for weeks. Maybe since the day I dropped you off at the airport in Aruba."

He was moving his hips in and out of her slow and steady. Teasing her almost as he talked.

"What was that?" she asked, her breath catching.

Her eyes were glued to his, searching and trying to read something she might not believe.

If he was in her shoes he could understand that and might doubt the words too.

He was going to do whatever he could to get her to believe him though.

"That I love you. That I've never really loved anyone other than family and yet what I feel for you could be classified as much more than that."

She blinked a few times, her eyes filling with light tears.

He wasn't sure if that was good or bad.

"I'm in love with you too," she said. "I just didn't think this would happen in my life. Least of all with someone like you."

He let out his breath. He'd been holding that along with not moving his body.

He hadn't even realized he was frozen while he waited for her reply. Her response. A reaction.

Anything.

It was what he'd been hoping for.

"When did you know?" he asked.

"I don't know," she said. "I just did. I think I fought it and you wouldn't let me."

He smiled, his lips lowering to hers, their kiss getting deeper while his hips picked up speed.

There was a need building in him for a man wanting to show her how much of him she actually had.

How much she controlled.

Her hands were moving up and down his back, her legs lifting and going around his waist and holding him tight.

The bed couldn't move as it was bolted in place, but with the speed he was going, he wondered if he could shift it some.

Abby was getting loud and though he didn't worry anyone could hear, he continued to kiss her to cancel out the sounds they were making.

Her hands went to his ass, pushed him down and held him in place while she started to come.

He felt each and every pulse around his dick and all but

exploded making him think he could shoot right off of her with as hard as he was coming.

The two of them lay there holding each other for minutes until he finally rolled and had her on his chest.

"I should have said this to you weeks ago," he said.

She kissed him on the lips. "I'm not sure I would have been ready to hear it. I think you do things with the right timing even if you don't think you do."

She didn't say she wouldn't have felt it weeks ago, just that she might not be ready.

"Why are you ready now?" he asked.

"Because you're giving me time," she said. "I don't like to be pushed and you understand that. I know it's hard for you, but you're still doing it. Any other man might have just thrown in the towel and thought I was playing some game. I'm not."

"I know you're not," he said. "You're just not trusting."

"No," she said. "That's hard for me."

He wanted to ask if she trusted him, but he was afraid of the hurt if she'd said no and decided to take this win while he could.

26

WITHOUT ANY DISTRACTIONS

"Hi, Laken," Abby said on Saturday morning a few weeks later.

She'd flown to West's last night and they stayed at the penthouse. She wasn't a fan of staying in the city, but they were private in his place.

He'd taken her out to dinner last night. A late dinner. She'd put on a sundress and heeled sandals, West's driver took her to his office where she waited in the car for him to come out and then they went to dinner.

It was so far removed from when they'd met in Aruba. Still a sundress but the one there was casual. This one, she'd gone out to buy and hoped it was nice enough.

He'd brought up going to dinner after work and she knew he'd be dressed more professionally.

Sure, he'd removed his jacket and tie, but just his shirt and pants, shoes. The whole combination probably cost more than half her wardrobe.

If she didn't feel as if she measured up while they were out, she kept it to herself. Not much she could do and she sure the heck wasn't allowing West to buy her clothes.

He'd made a few comments about taking her shopping in the past and she'd shut him down in a New York minute.

The shocked look on his face was enough for him not to ask again.

But they got through the night, her eating dinner at close to eight, which she never did. She wasn't even hungry at that point, but again, his life was just different than hers.

This morning they were up bright and early and at the airport waiting for his siblings to arrive, with their flight leaving around nine. They'd be at his mother's by noon, she'd been told. There would be dinner tonight and they'd fly home tomorrow.

It just seemed like a lot to her, but she supposed it was no different than the average person did for a holiday and drove a few hours to get there for a party or a wedding.

"Good to see you again," Laken said. "I'm glad you were willing to do this. Did West warn you about our mother?"

She turned to look at West, his head popping up from his phone. He'd been on it a lot and she imagined things were going on with work, but he was trying to get it out of the way so that they could focus while they were together.

Like he'd told her more than once he was trying to do.

"No," she said. "What do I have to worry about?"

"Nothing," West said. "My mother is pushy. I told you how she got the whole family together for this before I got the call."

She grinned. "I find it sweet."

"Good," Laken said. "Here comes Foster. Braylon is always the last one."

She saw Foster walking through the door of the private suite they were in at the airport.

"Is Susie going to be on the flight and staying too?" she asked.

"Yes," he said. "Her husband is flying with her. They are on the plane already. Their kids are with friends for the weekend and the two of them are going to take a short mini weekend away."

"That's nice of you," she said.

It must have been the tone of her voice that had Laken laughing.

"West is a nice guy but doesn't show it often."

"She has to go anyway and she has a hotel for the night," he said. "It costs nothing for her husband to go and gives her something to do while she waits for us to return. No reason for her and the pilots to return here and then fly back to get us tomorrow."

"I still find it nice that you give those kinds of benefits to your employees," she said. Abby knew a lot of bosses didn't do that. She worked for some at her job that didn't even want to associate with anyone below them.

"I'm not late," Braylon said, walking through the door. "Get that look off your face, Laken."

She grinned over the two siblings. "You're always the last one," Laken said.

"But still not late," West said. "We've got ten minutes before we have to board, twenty before we are cleared for takeoff, if not more."

His head went back down to his phone.

"What's going on?" Braylon asked and moved closer. "I got your text this morning."

"We'll talk on the plane," he said.

"It's Saturday," Laken said. "I thought you didn't work when you were with Abby."

"It's fine," she said. "I understand things can happen."

"It happens more than you think," Foster said. "I'm surprised it hasn't before now."

Laken had moved over by West and Braylon and they were talking. Foster stayed a few seats away from where she'd walked to when West's siblings joined him. She'd give them privacy. It didn't concern her and she didn't care all that much.

She and West spent last night together without any distractions. A few hours wasn't the end of the world. She was positive his mother was going to be on his case to not be working so she didn't want to come off as the bad guy.

"I know he's a busy man," she said. "Just like you all are. I mean, not one of you is in a relationship, right? There has to be a reason for it."

Foster snorted. He was the quietest, she'd heard from West. The one always doing his own thing.

"We all seem to have a problem prioritizing."

"Maybe it's time your older brother shows you how it's done," she said primly.

Foster grinned. "You're good for him. I hope he appreciates it and that you have patience."

She didn't get a chance to ask what that meant when Susie came in and said they could all board.

She went to grab her bag, but West had it. They'd packed together and it was only one night. She was nervous about this and what to wear, but he'd told her it was casual. Only family. Not to stress.

When West put shorts and a T-shirt on, she'd relaxed some. She'd put on tan shorts, a flowery printed shirt that was soft and feminine and a pair of sandals on her feet.

Everyone was in shorts, Laken even in jean shorts. Guess West was right about it being casual.

When they were all seated on the plane and given the all clear for takeoff, the siblings were still talking about work and some venture that West was buying and it was now being held up. Something about backgrounds not coming back the way he wanted.

When the seatbelt light went off, she undid hers and moved over to the lounge area and turned the TV on. Susie was with her husband chatting, so no reason to bug her. Foster was talking with his siblings having been pulled into whatever was going on.

She was going to entertain herself and not be a nuisance and try to keep Foster's words in her head. To be patient.

She'd been dating West now for over two months and most times he was a very attentive boyfriend when they were together.

Things happened and she knew that; she'd get over it for the two-hour flight there.

Less than two hours later, they were all back in their seats and the plane was descending. West leaned over. "Sorry," he said. "This came up last night and I didn't want to bother them knowing I'd see them today. I won't talk about it again."

"It's okay," she said. "I know you have to talk to Talia about her future. You're seeing Rowan, Elias and Nelson in person for the first time in months. I'm sure work will come up."

"Yeah," he said. "It will. It's hard not to. My mother will rein it in, but she knows how this goes. She has to take the good with the bad."

"I'm just glad we had last night together," she said.

His hand reached for hers and their fingers threaded together. "Me too."

When they were on the ground, she and West got in one car, Laken and Braylon another, Foster a third.

"Why are we all getting in different cars?" she asked. "I

thought we were going to your mom's. Isn't everyone staying there tonight?"

She hadn't had a chance to even ask that. She knew his mother's house was big and probably had enough room.

"No, we aren't staying there. Not everyone is. Foster is going to Elias's later. He's probably on his way to my Mom's now since it'd be out of his way to go to Elias's first and then come back. Laken and Braylon are going to my Mom's and then staying there. Talia still lives there. Rowan and Nelson will stay at a hotel because they will go out tonight."

"You've never said, who is close to who? I mean, I know your sisters are pretty far apart in age."

"They are," he said. "Not very close either, but Laken tries. Foster and Elias are close. They have similar personalities. Even though Rowan and Elias are just a year apart, Rowan and Nelson get along better."

"I'm not sure I could keep track of it all," she said. "I'm glad it's just me and Liz."

"And you're close with your sister."

"Are you the closest with Braylon?" she asked. "I'm just guessing that since you work together."

And also since West had told her Braylon stuck with his older brother right after college when he could have moved on to other things.

"Yes," he said.

He didn't say anymore and she wasn't sure why. There was part of her that didn't think West got that close with anyone. She thought maybe she was the exception, but today didn't seem like that.

"Are you nervous for some reason?" she asked.

"No," he said, turning his head. "Why?"

"You're distracted," she said. "Or is it work?"

"Sorry," he said, sighing. "Just a lot on my mind."

She nodded and let it go. Again, she had to get used to this even though she'd told him before that she didn't want to be a second-class person.

He hadn't shown her much of that until today so she'd let it go as a one-time thing.

"No worries," she said. "You didn't tell me where we were staying. At a hotel too?"

"No," he said. "You'll see when we get there."

It wasn't that long of a drive. Fifteen minutes and they pulled into a really small ranch. The outside was brick, there was no garage and his rental went into the driveway that looked new.

The shutters were painted black and looked fresh.

"You rented a house?"

"This is the house we moved to after my father died," he said. "The nine of us lived here after we moved from Fort Bragg. Well, Fort Liberty now."

She knew the name had changed a few years ago. West had explained that to her too.

"You kept this house?" she asked.

They walked up the stairs. The house was next to others like it and not private at all like his house in the Hamptons.

"I did," he said. "I had work done to it and it's available for any of the family to stay at when they come visit if they don't want to stay with our mother. Since you're with me, it's ours. Normally Braylon would have come too."

"He could have," she said.

"Nope," he said. "He didn't even ask because he knows the answer."

She found it both sweet and sentimental that West kept the home they'd lived in after their father died.

When he opened the door she saw how small the place was.

The living room was closed off to any other room but a doorway that led to a hall and one to a room she assumed was the dining room.

"How did you all fit in this house? How many bedrooms are there?"

He laughed. "We were tight. Three bedrooms and one and a half baths back then. My mother, Laken, and Talia shared a room. Me, Braylon, and Foster another. Then Elias, Rowan and Nelson the last. Things got shifted as we all moved out. I mean, I was in college shortly after we moved here, so I only was here on breaks."

She couldn't imagine the cramped living quarters.

"Is this room the biggest?" she asked.

"No," he said. "But it has the attached half bath. My mother and the girls were in here. I think it made sense my mother got a little privacy and didn't have to share with six boys. Though there was only one shower."

She shivered. "How did you all get ready?"

"The younger ones showered or bathed at night. The rest of us jumped in and out fast. Boys are easy, not a lot to do to get ready."

She shook her head. "So this is your room now when you stay here?"

"It's anyone's room they want but nice to have the bath. It's got a shower in there now. When I had work done to it, I had them take some space from the room to put it in. This way, more than one person can stay here and be out of the way."

"You really did put your family first," she said, putting her arms around him. "Do you ever put yourself first?"

"I am now," he said softly. "Or at least hope you see that I'm trying."

She didn't normally see West looking vulnerable and

wouldn't bring it up either. "I do," she said and kissed him. "We've got time before we get to your Mom's right? How about you show me how much you're trying."

He laughed and picked her up, then put her on the king-sized bed that was squeezed into the room.

27

HE WANTED MORE

A little over an hour later, West and Abby were pulling into his mother's long driveway of the big house he'd had built for her years ago.

It was more space than she needed by the time he could afford it, but he wanted to make sure that all the kids still living at home had their own rooms since no one did when he was younger.

He went back to that home when he visited and hoped it humbled him at times.

But today, he wanted Abby to have a reminder that he wasn't much different than her at the heart of it.

In the past few weeks he'd felt as if he was ignoring her and hated it.

There was part of him that was getting into old habits he had to break and the other part that was scared at how fast he was moving with her and knowing she didn't seem to be keeping up.

It was better for him to focus on work than on the fact she was hours away and didn't seem as if she was going to move anytime soon.

Not that they'd had those conversations, but he knew enough not to bring them up.

They loved each other and that was a good start. It's just...he wanted more.

"Is everyone here?" she asked when she got out of his rental.

"I think Nelson's flight is arriving soon. I'm sure Rowan went to get him. Rowan came in last night since he was furthest away."

"Is everyone leaving tomorrow?" she asked.

"No," he said. "Laken is flying out Monday from here and going right to Utah for work. Braylon and Foster are returning with us. I'm not sure about Nelson or Rowan. They normally stay a little longer, but again, we didn't talk much about it."

He didn't care all that much and it's not like anyone shared their travel plans. He only knew what he did because his mother informed him.

He opened the front door and his mother was right there with a big grin on her face.

She didn't look fifty-six to him. She still looked like she had when his father died, eighteen years ago, only with a different hairstyle.

He wondered now why she never tried to date again. It was not a conversation he'd ever had and he wasn't sure if anyone else did either.

She was still young back then, but again, she had eight kids from ages four to eighteen. He was positive she had no time and probably thought no one would want that headache.

They sure were a handful at times.

"There is my oldest," his mother said, giving him a big hug. "Abby. It's so nice to meet you in person."

His mother turned and pulled his girlfriend into her arms. "It's nice to meet you too."

Abby was laughing and returned the hug easily. He should have warned her about that, but she didn't seem to mind.

"You're so lovely in person. I can see where West would have come to your aid and defense when you first met."

"He told me I reminded him some of Talia."

He heard a laugh and turned to his youngest sister. "I don't think West would have done that to me. He would have walked in and gotten in the guy's face and said hands off and then told him what would happen if the guy didn't leave."

"I don't use violence," he argued.

"Now," his mother said. "But you could get West riled when he was younger. Not that he had a short fuse, but when he lost it, boy, you had to watch out. And West, you should have introduced Talia and Abby. Don't make it look as if I didn't raise you to have manners."

His mother took care of the introductions before he could. It's not like he even had a chance to do it anyway.

"This is interesting," Abby said. "I would have never guessed that you riled easily."

"I'm not that person," he said. "Not anymore. I don't need another reputation more than the one I've got."

"What reputation is that?" Abby asked.

"That West is ruthless when it comes to business," Talia said. "We know he's not, but most times people don't want to be bought out. Or it's not their first choice."

"I bet it's more that West just keeps to himself and doesn't let a lot of people in to get to know him."

"I love you already," his mother said. "Please, come in. I've got snacks out. I was going to cook, but West told me no way. He never lets me do too much when we are all together. I had it catered though I hate that. I did make some desserts."

"Mom," he said.

His mother had slaved over them for years. There was no reason for it now.

"Stop it," his mother said. "I can make cookies. I made four different kinds. Enough that everyone has a few choices. Cookies are easy and fun. It's not like I've got a ton to do with my time anymore with you all grown up and out but Talia."

"And I'm going to be out soon," Talia said.

"We'll talk about it later," West said. He didn't want to get his hand slapped. "Abby, my brothers, Rowan and Elias."

Abby moved forward and shook both of his other brothers' hands.

"Nice to meet you," Rowan said. "Hate to rush, but I need to go get Nelson. He's landing in thirty."

His brother left and he and Abby went out to the deck where Laken, Braylon and Foster were seated.

"Can I get you something to drink?" his mother asked Abby.

"I'll get it," West said, getting back up. "Do you want tea or water?"

He knew what she drank most times.

"Water is good," she said. "Thanks."

He left his girlfriend to talk to his siblings and hoped his mother would have stayed, but she followed him to the kitchen.

"What's wrong with you?" his mother asked.

"Nothing, why?"

"I thought you'd be smiling more. Laken says you're

almost a different person and yet you seem distant right now. Are things not good with Abby?"

"They are fine," he said. "I've just got a lot on my mind with work."

"I heard," his mother said. "Braylon and Laken were talking about it and now you can stop. It's not the end of the world and nothing you can do. You're here to visit with your siblings and I want the work talk to a minimum."

"You know that is impossible. I've got to find out what is going on with Talia. Is she still talking about moving out?"

"I'm sure you'll hear her idea in a few minutes," his mother said. "I told her no, but she won't listen to me. It has to come from you."

"You told me months ago I'm not her father, so I'm not telling her no."

He didn't need to get lectured again.

"You'll see why when she asks. I'm letting her do it. I know you'll talk about work, but I ask that you don't do it the whole time. I want to know more about Abby."

"I've told you things," he said.

"You're a guy. You don't know the things to ask. Watch and learn."

His mother walked out after that and all he could do was follow with two bottles of water. He wanted a beer, but he'd hold off a bit since it seemed no one else was drinking yet.

"Abby," his mother said. "West said you've got one older sister. Liz, right?"

"Yes," she said. "She's seven years older than me. She helped raise me at times."

"Oh," his mother asked, looking at him. He hadn't given his mother details about Abby's upbringing. He didn't think it was his place.

"My mother left when I was younger," she said. "My

father raised us. Liz helped. My father owns his own fencing company so he worked a lot during nicer weather. But he's great. Best father ever."

He noticed Abby didn't provide any more details about her mother and he wouldn't either. Not that his mother wouldn't ask him the minute she had a chance. He'd tell her it was none of her business.

"I hope my children say I'm the best mother ever," his mother said. "There is nothing better in the world than to hear that, if you ask me."

"You've got your moments," he said, grinning.

"Hey," Talia said. "Mom is great. I know I probably got more individual attention than the rest of you, but you don't know her like I do."

"I didn't have time to let anyone get to know me like you, Talia. It's probably why you and I fight as much. You know more than you should. You're a bit intrusive."

Talia could be that way. He often wondered if maybe his baby sister did get spoiled more.

Not just by his mother but also by him and everyone else.

Talia didn't know what it was like to want for much in life. She was too young to remember the struggles that the rest of them had.

"I just ask questions," Talia said. "That is how you find things out." His sister turned to Abby. "What do you think of West as a boyfriend? I mean you're the first person he's brought home for everyone to meet. If Mom hadn't pushed this, I'm not sure he would have done it."

He felt his face fill with heat. That question might not have come out the way Talia wanted, but it was more than he wanted said.

The last thing he needed was for Abby to feel as if he wasn't going to introduce her to people.

Before he could argue, Abby said, "I think he's a good boyfriend, all things considered with our distance." There was some laughter there. "I'm sorry. I'll explain. I've got a family and friends, not to mention a job. He has a job and a family. Not so sure about friends, but he probably has no time. I can't be with him every weekend just like I'm sure he has things to do. But when we are together, he makes the time for me. Most times."

She was grinning. "I apologized for today," he said.

"And there was no need. Things happen," she said. "You always make it up to me."

Abby winked at him and his mother laughed. "I think you're just what West needs in his life to not let him think he can control it all. I'm to blame for that. He had a lot on his shoulders early on. Even when I told him to cut it out, he didn't listen. He got that from his father."

Every once in a while his mother would compare him to his father.

Some ways it made him feel great.

Others like shit.

He knew his father had an important job to do, but he felt it was selfish that his father stayed in the service as long as he had and left his kids and wife home.

It only reminded him that he wasn't there much for Abby.

Sure, what she said was true. And the fact they didn't live by each other made it worse.

But if she lived with him, they wouldn't have this problem.

"Your husband had to be a wonderful man," Abby told

his mother. "And it looks to me like you did a great job raising your children."

"All but Talia," Elias said, grinning.

"Not funny," Talia said. At five years apart, Elias would have been one of the brothers keeping his sister protected for years. He was the only one still close by to do it and West knew Elias had stepped up to the task more than once.

"No," Elias said. "It wasn't funny to get calls from Mom that you were dating some loser and that I needed to talk to him."

"How come I didn't know that?" West asked.

"Because you were too far away," his mother said. "There is more than one man in this family."

"Speaking of family and all," Talia said. "Can I move into the old house? I want my own space. I won't have to get roommates to pay for it. It's paid for. I mean I'll pay all the utilities and such, but there is no rent. You own it."

His baby sister was trying to send him a sweet grin to get him to give in.

"No," he said simply. "It's not for you. It's for everyone."

"But there is more than enough room here for people to stay when they visit," Talia argued.

"Not everyone wants to stay with Mom if they've got a significant other with them," Braylon said.

"Like any of you has ever brought anyone home," Talia said.

"Now that West has," his mother said. "Maybe others will too."

He watched his siblings all look at each other and then to him and Abby.

"We got played," Foster said.

West laughed. "I'm glad to know you are all catching on to how Mom operates."

His mother laughed. "You guys are all so easy. Who wants snacks? The caterers did too nice of a job making them pretty. It's just food to be eaten."

"I'll help," Talia said, standing up. His youngest sister was frowning. She wouldn't argue over the house, but she wasn't happy.

"We'll talk before I leave, Talia. We'll figure something out that works for everyone. In the meantime, you've got the whole basement as your living quarters. It's not like you're in Mom's way or the other way around."

"I know," Talia said. "It's just, I want to move on like you all did."

"Then figure it out," Laken said. "Saying it is one thing, but you can't expect to take steps if you don't know the direction you're going in."

"You've worked with West way too long," Talia said to Laken. "You all have. I feel like Rowan and I and Elias are the ones that just have more of a carefree life because we don't report daily."

Elias snorted. "Who says I've got a life outside of work?"

West looked at Elias, shaking his head. He knew his brother spent more time than most at his business because he was driven to be the best. Brewing took time to get a name and his brother was determined to get it to work his way.

He couldn't complain in the least with the revenue coming in, even if what Elias was doing wasn't the way he'd set up the business.

Talia had left the room to help his mother.

"Don't listen to her. Rowan has always danced to his own beat. But at least he's focused," Braylon said. "Working with you daily doesn't make us a different person than we've always been."

He appreciated that Braylon came to his defense, but he didn't need it.

"No one likes to be compared to another," Abby said. "Lots of people did it to Liz and me. I'm just more sensitive than her and have always been that way. I doubt any of you are like West just because you spend time with him. Maybe you are the opposite because of it."

Abby was grinning.

"Could be," he said. "I'd like to think everyone has a voice and a choice. It's what they choose to do with them."

He was looking at Abby when he said that. She dipped her head down but didn't say anything else.

28

EVERYDAY NORMAL PERSON

A t the end of July, Abby felt like things were going well.

If she found it odd that West's mom was texting her more than her boyfriend was, she didn't say a word.

Maybe she found comfort in the fact that Aileen accepted her into the family so easily.

There were times that she and Aileen would talk about West and if he was eating well or Aileen would just ask her how her job was going. If she had a good day or week.

Motherly things she'd never gotten growing up.

The things she'd always wanted and got to see when she visited Fayetteville earlier in the month and met all of West's family.

The interactions between the big family were funny and serious.

There were laughs and joking and lots of memories shared.

West also was firm with his sister Talia to get something to focus on and then they could talk about the next step.

He wasn't mean. He didn't even lecture. He also gave options.

He didn't ask Talia what she wanted. Just told her to figure it out and get back to him.

Abby might not have thought much of it other than it seemed like that was how the two of them worked too. She knew she had a voice, yet he never asked her to give it.

Maybe she should find some courage to speak up a bit more.

She found it ironic in a way that Talia was given choices when at twenty-two she was all about finding a job. The first job she could find so that she could have money and be an adult.

She did see Talia wanting to be an adult, but the money motivation didn't seem to be there.

Though she knew that West wanted his siblings to have a life he didn't have, she wondered if it wasn't helping his two youngest in the least.

It wasn't just Talia, but Nelson that also seemed to be expecting things without working for it.

She kept those opinions to herself though. Even when West's mother brought up the other siblings, she only listened and never contributed. She didn't want to be caught in the middle of anything.

Just like she wasn't bringing it up to West that she'd overheard him telling Foster that he was hoping he could convince her to move to the Hamptons. That she could work with Foster or any of his companies. She could go to Manhattan with him daily or work remotely. He'd find her something.

She ground her teeth when she heard that but never said a word. Again, he stated something without even talking to her, let alone asking.

Maybe it was just talk and he didn't mean it. Even Foster laughed and told him he was rushing.

When there was a knock at her office door, she turned her head to see a coworker standing there. "Hi, Carly. What can I help you with?"

Carly was a few years older than her and engaged. She suspected the department gossip was here to chat and not work.

"I just saw this on a website," Carly said. "Tell me this isn't you."

"What?" she asked, reaching for Carly's phone. It was some blog or gossip article. And at the top was a picture of her and West out to dinner weeks ago. The Friday before they left for his mother's.

The headline read, "Billionaire Finds Himself A Gold Digger, Or Is It A Cinderella Story?"

She hadn't thought if any of West's siblings considered her a gold digger. That hadn't crossed her mind. But now that this was out in the news, everyone was going to think that.

"Is that really you?" Carly asked. "Your name isn't listed. Just that picture. Though these stories start that way and I'm waiting for the next one to come out with more information."

She wasn't listening to Carly but was reading the article that had more information on her than she wanted.

No, her name wasn't given, but they alluded to the long-distance relationship. That it had been going on for months and that the mysterious woman was just an everyday normal person.

She laughed over what she thought was a compliment.

Her whole life she wanted to be thought of as normal and never felt she was. Or that she was looked at that way.

Now the bigger question was how to answer Carly.

If she said it wasn't her, then Carly wouldn't believe her or make some joke and she hated to lie.

If she said it was her, the whole building would know in minutes.

Correction, the whole building was going to know in minutes whether she admitted it or not.

She didn't have a chance to even answer when her cell phone rang.

Saved.

Or not when she saw it was West calling. Which meant he had to have seen this too because he never called her during the day.

It was barely nine on a Tuesday on top of it.

"I'm sorry," she said. "I need to take this. Can you give me privacy?"

Carly frowned at her, but she waved her out, then got up and shut her door.

"I need to give you a heads up," West said before she even said hello.

"I think I know," she said.

"What do you know?" he asked.

"What is it you wanted to tell me?"

Best to let him say it first.

"There is an article that was released about thirty minutes ago with a picture of you and me in it."

"I saw it," she said.

"You did?" he asked.

"My coworker Carly must read those things. She came to me and wanted to know if it was me. I read the article and you called before I could answer. I'm sure she's running around the building right now asking everyone's opinion. What do I do? It doesn't say my name."

"The next article released in an hour or so will," he said. "Huh?"

"Abby. That is how it works. One outlet releases and hints at things, the rest are scrambling to get more. The second article will come out with your name and then it just builds. Someone will find out where you work. They will get your number. They are going to want comments and ask questions."

She let out a sigh. "I doubt that. I mean come on, it says I'm an everyday normal person."

There was silence on the other line. "That's why they are going to hound you. If you were from my world you'd know how to handle this. They are going to think you don't. That you have no shield in front of you."

She didn't like that he'd just said she wasn't from his world when he tried so hard to tell her she was.

She didn't want her eyes to fill with tears and be sensitive to that. He was probably just stressed over this.

Or maybe he was embarrassed.

"What do you want me to do?" she asked. "Deny it's me?"

"God, no," he said. "I can't believe it lasted as long as it had with no one figuring it out. I could say that it was a business meeting, but my guess is there are multiple pictures of us. If they were following us that weekend, they know we got on the plane with Laken and Braylon. My secretary has been fielding calls left and right. It's best to get in front of this."

"You're making it sound like a bad thing," she said quietly.

"I don't want it to be," he said. "It's not for me. Not at all. I just don't want you to make any decisions based on what might happen for a few weeks."

"Few weeks?" she asked.

"I'm hoping it will blow over by then," he said. "Something juicier will come around. But my point is, I know this isn't what you wanted. You didn't want to be the center of attention and this is more than my family asking intrusive questions."

Abby grinned over his dry tone. He'd gotten annoyed at some of the questions asked of her a few weeks ago, but she wasn't offended. She was just positive no one questioned West on anything.

She was glad that he at least remembered earlier on she said she didn't want all this attention or her name out there. She supposed that by continuing with the relationship though, she gave him the impression she was fine if it happened.

"Tell me what to say and do," she said. "I'll make sure my father and sister know. I don't want them hounded. Do you think more will come out?"

"Yes," he said. "Tell your coworker that it is you. Don't lie about anything. That will only make things worse. Say we met in Aruba if anyone asks."

"It's the truth," she said.

"That's right. The truth is what I'm saying. But I'm not giving a lot of facts."

"I don't want to give facts," she said. "It's no one's business."

"It's not," he said. "But if you give a little they will go away. That's all I'm saying. For now, I'm not speaking to anyone. That's normal for me. I've got people to take those calls for me. I've got ways to avoid it."

"But I don't," she said. There was no one here to protect her as he'd said.

She didn't have a helicopter she could get on the roof of

the building. Or a driver that she could sneak out a back-door to meet. None of those things. Not even her own home where she could avoid people either.

"Can you take some time off and come here?" he asked.

"No," she said. "I mean I've got time, but I don't want to waste it for this. It's not like I can run forever. I don't want to live like that."

There was silence after those words. She didn't know how he was going to take it, but she had to let it go for now.

"You won't be," he said. "If you can just send me a text any time you talk to someone, I'd appreciate it."

"What?" she asked. "I don't report to you. I'm not going to text you every time someone asks me a question about my boyfriend."

He sighed. "I don't mean it that way. I meant if someone reaches out to ask questions that you don't know."

"Oh," she said. "Yes, I can do that."

"I've got lawyers on hand to deal with anything that is false. I just want to get ahead of it."

"Can I ask who they are and where they are calling from?" she asked.

"Of course you can," he said. "And if you want to reply with no comment, that is your choice too."

She wouldn't though unless he asked her to. But he didn't. He actually sounded like he *wanted* her to admit it.

Was he going to use this as an excuse to get their relationship out in the open?

She never thought he was hiding it. He'd been fast to have her meet his siblings that first weekend.

And though it was said more than once that West might not have brought her home to meet his mother if he wasn't manipulated by it, she didn't believe that.

She'd met Aileen already with a video call. She found it

funny how Aileen worked her kids around each other and they didn't seem to notice it half the time.

"I'll keep you posted," she said.

"Abby," he said. "I love you. Just remember that and give me and this a chance. Don't let it get in your head."

"I love you too," she said. "And I'll try not to."

She hung up the phone and then opened her door.

There was Carly standing there with three more people in their department.

"Well?" Carly said. "It's you, right? We all think it."

Abby was going to go with her gut and that meant saying the truth but limiting it.

"It is me."

"You're dating a billionaire?" Carly asked, her jaw dropping. "For how long?"

"A few months," she said.

"Was that him that just called you? West, his name is?"

"It is West and that was him," she said.

"Where would you meet someone like him?" Diane asked. She was younger than Abby and had been hired about six months ago. She was glued to Carly and always asking questions about people.

It was the "someone like him" comment that got to her. She didn't need to be reminded she'd never be good enough for West.

"We met in Aruba," she said.

More jaws were dropping over that. "You had a vacation fling?" Carly asked.

"Since we are dating and have been, I'd hardly say it was a fling."

"Why are you still working here?" Diane asked. "I'd go work with him and get out of here. Or not work at all."

"I have a job and a life and family here," she argued.

"Would any of you pick up your life and move after dating someone for only a few months? This is no different. Now if you'll excuse me, I've got work to do."

She turned and shut her door to get back to work. Though West told her she didn't have to let him know every time she talked to someone, she wanted him to know what she'd said right now.

Maybe this would be a subtle hint for him to not get anything in his head right now about her uprooting her life any more than it was.

29

LEARN TO DEAL

Abby said she'd try not to let it get in her head, but West knew it was going to.

"How did she sound?" Braylon asked him when he looked at the phone in his hand after he'd hung up.

"Confused," he said. "Nervous. Maybe scared. I can't protect her here. I should go to her."

"No," Braylon said. "You did and said all the right things to her. You don't need to be there for her. She needs to deal with this on her own and get used to it."

He frowned. "No, she doesn't. What if she decides she doesn't want to and ends things?"

Braylon shook his head. "That is why she needs to learn to deal with it without you holding her hand. If you run to her aid the first time it happens, she's not going to be able to handle it on her own. Didn't you, Laken, and I talk about this with Talia and Nelson just recently? That they've had it too easy and now expect everything handed to them?"

"That has nothing to do with Abby. She hasn't had

anything easy in her life and nothing handed to her," he argued.

"That isn't what I meant," Braylon said.

"Then what did you mean?"

"I mean if she's strong enough to put up with you, then she should be strong enough to handle this. Give it a few days. Be by her side. Make time for her when she texts and calls, but don't rush there and put lawyers and everything else in front of her. That will only add more fuel to the fire and maybe piss her off that you don't think she can handle it."

"There is no fire. I've got a girlfriend. Big fucking deal."

"That's right," Braylon said. "Not a big deal, but if you are acting like it is, everyone is going to wonder more and she's going to think she has no say or control. Do you want that?"

He wasn't used to other people telling him what to do.

"Find out everything you can."

"You want me to do a dive into Abby?" Braylon asked, looking stunned. "Why now? Did you not hear what I just said?"

"No!" he snapped. "Not her. I know everything."

"I doubt that," Braylon said, snorting. "No one knows everything."

He waved his hand. "I know what I need to know. She's an open book."

He didn't feel anything was shocking in Abby's life. She'd been open from the first time they'd met.

She wore her emotions on her face. Kind of like Talia did. Only different.

"Then what do you want me to find out?" Braylon asked.

"This article. Find out what more they've got. You know

as well as I do there is more. Pictures, comments, assumptions."

"Tell me anything you know about Abby that I should be aware of so I'm not blindsided."

He didn't want to tell his brother about Abby's mother, but maybe he should.

"I want you on this and only this right now. Do you hear me?"

"Yes," Braylon said. "This isn't my first time around dealing with these things."

He'd had other shit written about him in the past.

Never a woman he'd been with. Most times he'd get a heads up first that something was coming out. As if a news site wanted to be bought to not air it.

This time, no one came to him first.

If they had, he would have taken care of it. That was what was concerning him the most. Why no one approached him with this information.

Was he happy that their relationship was out in the open? Yeah, he was.

Maybe he had to look at it as Braylon said and see how Abby handled this.

She'd said more than once her father tried to protect her and now she was still paying for not being told things earlier on. It was best if he didn't follow suit.

"Fine," he said. "You heard Abby say her mother left when she was a child. She's in a supportive housing facility right now. She's got some mental health and addiction issues that she's been battling for years. I believe she's in a good spot right now, but it's been up and down all of Abby's life. They aren't close and I'm not sure they ever will be."

"That's too bad," Braylon said. "She talks fondly of her sister and father."

"She has a great relationship with them. There isn't anything about Abby that is a secret. The person who wrote this article must know who she is."

"I'm sure they've got her name and are just teasing with it," Braylon said. "The whole Cinderella or Gold Digger comment. It's a joke. No one thinks that. And trust me, there have been some in the past when Mom did think that."

He snorted. "I've never dated anyone seriously enough for her to feel that way."

"Nope," Braylon said. "And if you did, Mom would have put her foot down. She has no problem telling you what she is thinking."

"Yet she never did with anyone else," he said.

It's not that he didn't date. He just didn't date seriously.

"She would talk to me about it," Braylon said. "Just like she talks to you about me. It's how she does it. Always."

"She's sneaky that way," he said.

"She's never going to change. It's the way she is. I hear she talks to Abby a lot."

"What?" he asked. Why was this news to him?

"Never mind," Braylon said.

"Oh no," he said. "I want to hear this."

He wasn't sure why Abby never said a word.

"It's nothing," Braylon said. "I'm hearing it from Laken, which means Mom must tell her."

West picked his phone up and called his sister. She answered on the second ring. "Are you in the building?"

"Yes," Laken said. "But I've got a meeting in fifteen minutes."

"Come to my office," he said and hung up.

"That was rude," Braylon said.

"It will get her here. She'll think it's work related and rush."

"You're just as sneaky as Mom is. If you said it had to do with Mom calling Abby she'd hang up on *you*."

"That's right," he said.

It wasn't two minutes before Laken was pushing his door open. "What do you need? I've got a meeting."

"You can be late for your meeting if you are meeting with me. Talking to me is more important," he said, smirking.

He saw her look at Braylon and see the grin on his face.

"What's going on?" Laken asked.

"I'm sure you didn't see this," Braylon said, turning his computer around.

"Shit," Laken said. "I guess it took longer than I figured it would."

Laken read the article.

"That was my thought," he said. "I'm fine with it. I just talked to Abby."

"Let her handle it on her own," Laken said.

He lifted an eyebrow. "Why?"

"She has to figure it out. You can't save her from everything even though I know you want to."

"You know this because Mom told you that she talks to Abby?" he asked.

"Snitch," Laken said, looking at Braylon.

"I thought he knew. This is getting too confusing for me," Braylon said. "I'm going to be like Foster and just hide."

"You wouldn't survive a week with no one around you," he said. Braylon liked people too much. He could take a break but it never lasted.

"He obviously didn't. Which means Abby doesn't tell him everything. Good for her. It's not like Abby says much. It drives Mom nuts."

He crossed his arms. "Do you know what they are talking about?" he asked.

"It's Mom. She's being a mother. She asks things and Abby never really gives answers. I'm sure Mom tells stories about you as a kid too. It's not like they talk daily. Maybe a few times a week Mom texts her. Mom always starts it."

"That's good at least."

"I think Mom feels sorry for her," Laken said.

"Why?"

"Because anyone could see the longing in Abby's eyes when we were all together. We find it annoying at times, but she was all smiles. Abby said she didn't have a mother much in her life. Maybe she is just looking at things she missed. No clue."

Which meant if it was made public about Lily then his whole family would know and he should inform them now.

"I should tell you about Abby's mother."

When he was done saying the brief summary like he'd told Braylon, Laken said, "That's sad. It had to be hard too. I mean you know how hard it was not having a father around being a guy, but I had you guys. I'm glad Abby had Liz."

"Me too," he said. "Anyway, I'm going to have to let Mom know what is going on. She'll find out soon. Braylon, get to what I asked you."

His brother got up to leave, Laken moving to the door. "Am I dismissed now?" she asked sarcastically.

"Yes," he said, laughing. When his phone went off and he saw the text from Abby, he read it and smiled.

"Everything okay?" Braylon asked.

"Just Abby telling me how she handled it with her coworkers. She did well."

"Then let her continue to do well," Laken said.

When his phone rang next, his shoulders dropped. "Mom?" Braylon asked.

West sighed. "Yes. Let me handle this."

His siblings left laughing and he answered his phone. "How dare someone say that about Abby?" his mother all but screamed into the phone. "They better not call her a gold digger again."

His thought exactly. "They didn't," he said. "And they won't. Braylon is taking care of it. Abby is aware and we've talked. It's going to be fine."

"You're damn right it is," his mother said. "I'm going to talk to Braylon and find out some people's names and knock heads together."

He grinned. "No, you're not. There is no reason to get involved. It's not the first time my name has been in the news and it won't be the last."

His mother searched for all their names daily. She said it was to have a scrapbook type thing. He figured it had more to do with being nosy but whatever floated her boat.

"Abby has to be upset," his mother said. "She wouldn't like those negative things said about her."

"And you know this how?" he asked.

He wanted to see if his mother would admit to talking to his girlfriend.

"Anyone can see how sensitive she is to things. She's perfect for you."

"Because she's sensitive?" he asked.

"Because she makes you stop and think about your actions," his mother said. "I bet she's been doing that from the first day you met."

Damn his mother for understanding that.

From day one he was drawn to Abby because she reminded him of his sister. Then she made him feel and think things about his family that he'd forgotten or neglected.

Abby made him realize everything he was missing in life and how to find a way to get more of it now.

In the past he'd just do what he wanted. He'd make calls. He threw money around. He'd give orders.

No one told him no.

But Abby did.

She made him stop and think and not be an ass around her.

In that time, he wasn't trying to be an ass to his siblings either.

Though today Laken might not think it with the way he wanted her here. She'd understand now too because in the end, family always came first.

Abby reminded him of that too.

What she was going to find out soon was that she was considered family now.

30

FOREIGN CONCEPT

"How is the celebrity doing?" Liz asked Abby three weeks later.

"Not even funny," she said. It was Monday morning and she'd be leaving for work soon. Her sister stopped over quickly on her way out of work and home to sleep. "What are you doing here?"

"Just wanted to say hi," Liz said. "We haven't seen much of each other this summer. I'm off on the weekends and you're gone most of them. I work nights and you're working days."

She could have dinner with her sister during the week and that was what they used to do before, but with Liz living with Christian, she knew that was the only time the two of them saw each other and she wouldn't infringe on it.

"Sorry for not being around more," she said. "You could have said you wanted to spend time together. I mean we are getting things done for the wedding, but am I falling behind on anything?"

"No," Liz said. "It's not that."

Liz and Christian's wedding was less than three months

away. It was just going to be small. She had to all but twist her sister's arm to get a real wedding gown just because it was her second wedding.

"Then what is going on?" she asked.

"I wanted to see how you were doing in person. It's been a few weeks now since the news of your relationship came out with West. You're not used to being in the spotlight like that. Dad was worried."

"Everyone worried about nothing," she said. "It blew over fast enough."

West was right. There were a few articles that came out. They said her name, some background on her. They even posted her parents' names and her father's business, but not much about her mother.

"You said West was antsy over it," Liz said. "Why?"

She'd felt he was but got more of the information from Aileen. There was part of her that didn't like always talking to West's mother, but the other part loved it.

That she felt so welcomed into the family and she knew Aileen was just worried about West.

What a foreign concept to her. A mother being worried about their child.

"I think he was concerned that it would push me away," she said and turned her head.

"Are you having second thoughts about things now?" Liz asked, frowning. "I know you didn't sign up for all of this. And you said at work people were bugging you that first week, but it quieted down."

"No second thoughts. Not really. I mean I love him. He loves me. I believe that he does. There are weeks we don't talk much. I flew to him after this happened weeks ago, you know that. He wanted me away from it. He came to see me the weekend after, then I got home last night. It's just a lot."

"Too much?" Liz asked. "I know it's only been a few months. Do you think maybe he might want you to move there with him?"

She decided to tell her sister what she'd overheard over a month ago. "He hasn't brought it up. I'm glad. I'm not ready for that. It's way too soon to uproot my whole life for someone. I mean what if I moved there and it didn't work out? I've given up my job and my place."

Liz laughed. "You're talking to someone who did that and it didn't work out. I came home. I found another job and lived with Dad for a year. It wasn't ideal, but it happened and I'm not embarrassed over it. Or are you more worried that now that everyone knows, if you left and came back they'd know that too?"

She sighed. "It's crossed my mind."

"More than crossed it," Liz said. "Don't get into old habits of always worrying about things not working out rather than something that will. Not everyone leaves."

She didn't need her sister to remind her about those times she was afraid to let someone in. It seemed she was doing it again though.

"I know. But the chances of this working out are so slim. We are just two different people."

"No," Liz said. "You're not. Your careers are. You've told me more than once that his mother is so down to earth. His siblings seem to be too. No one is snooty, no one is looking down on anyone else. They all accepted you when they could have easily turned you away. His mother texts and calls you. Judy doesn't do that with me and I'm marrying her son."

Abby laughed. "Good point. I don't know how things are going to turn out. We haven't talked much about the future and I'm happy about that. I don't want to be pressured and

I'm not sure he's even thinking it. Overhearing that conversation with his brother could have just been talk to get me closer to him so he wasn't flying here. He knows it's hard on me to keep going every weekend to him. It's like during the week I'm running around to do everything I used to do on the weekends."

"I get it," Liz said. "You don't feel as if you've got a day to just be a bum."

She grinned. "Yeah. Stupid, I know. But when I'm there with him, I want to be with him. We don't have to go and do things, but he always wants to. I've finally got it in his head that when we are in the Hamptons, it's just us. I love it there. It's like living here but on the water with an awesome view. I can run to the store and no one knows me. It's like vacation in a way."

"Sounds like you wouldn't mind living there," Liz said.

"Who wouldn't want to live in that house?" she asked, laughing. "But I don't want to live off of him. I know I could find a job doing something. I like my job and when you look for a new one, you don't know what you'll get. It's not as if there are tons of HR jobs either."

"Valid arguments. Glad you haven't put much thought into it after just a few months."

She rolled her eyes at Liz's sarcastic tone. "I know. I'm all over the place. I need to just let it happen. Whatever that might be. Maybe if we talked about it more it'd be easier, but he doesn't bring it up so I won't."

She'd said she wasn't clingy and talking about their future just a few months in would contradict that.

"I'll get out of your way so you can get to work," Liz said. "Don't be afraid about calling or stopping over at night. Christian understands. It'd give him an excuse to find some other project to work on around the house."

"There is that," she said. "Thanks for being there for me. For always being there."

"You know it," Liz said. Her sister was getting ready to leave when her phone rang and she pulled it out of her purse. "It's Mom's facility. Hello? What? When? No, we haven't talked to her."

She was looking at her sister who was remaining calm, but inside, Abby's heart was racing. She'd just been waiting for this to happen again. Not that she knew what it was. "What's going on?" she asked.

Liz waved her hand at her to be quiet so she did while her sister finished the call. "Mom signed out yesterday and was supposed to be home last night and didn't return. The weekend staff wasn't paying much attention, but the program director came in this morning and started to worry. Mom said she was with us..."

Her shoulders dropped. "Why would she lie like that?"

"Abby."

"No," she said. "I don't want to believe she'd relapse."

"She has before. She could have again," Liz said. "Let's try to call her and see if we can figure out what is going on. Maybe she's just with friends and got held up."

"She would have called us if she was in trouble or needed a ride home," she argued. "She's done it before."

Months ago her mother had signed out for the weekend to be with friends and then couldn't get a ride back. Abby had driven the two hours to find where her mother was and brought her back. She'd worried her mother was using that weekend but hadn't seen any signs of it.

She did know her mother had been drinking, which wasn't allowed, but she suspected her mother stayed an extra day to sober up before she returned.

She'd decided to not tell Liz about the drinking. Her

mother denied it, but Abby wasn't an idiot.

She was calling her mother's phone, but it went to voice-mail. Liz was doing the same.

"I'm going to text her," Liz said.

"Me too," she said. "What should we do? Do we call the police?"

"Technically she hasn't been missing twenty-four hours and I'm sure they aren't going to do anything about it. She has a history of this. She's probably with friends and sleeping right now."

"I'll call into work. Do you know any of her friends? Should we go find out and talk to some people at the house or her roommate and see if they know where she is?"

"I'm sure they are doing that there. It's their job. The first thing they did was call us. They said they'd keep us posted," Liz said.

"I can't just sit around doing nothing," she said.

Liz sighed. "No. You can go to work and take your mind off of it. This is nothing new and you know it. What is different is that she came back into our lives and is exposing us to this again. She probably did this for years, but we just didn't know."

Her sister was right. "It doesn't change anything," she said.

"No," Liz said. "It doesn't. I'm going to make a few calls and then get some sleep. Go to work. I'll let you know if I find anything out."

Her sister was right. "I'll do that," she said.

But her mind wasn't on her job. She wanted to call West and tell him but then told herself he had more important things to worry about than his girlfriend's mother who had a history of disappearing with no explanation.

She was just thankful that none of her mother's past

came out in the articles and would embarrass West.

She'd even told him that and he brushed it off as if he didn't care one way or another. Maybe he didn't but *she* did.

Too many years of her life being talked about over Lily's actions was a shadow that trailed behind her even in the dark.

By one, her phone rang. It was Liz calling so she answered quickly. "Did they find Mom?"

"She's back," Liz said. "She showed up about thirty minutes ago. Abby, they drug tested her."

Her heart sank. "She was positive?"

"Yes. She broke the rules."

"Now what is going to happen?" she asked. "Are they kicking her out?"

"They wanted to. I talked to them and asked if they could hold her bed while we checked Mom back into rehab before this got out of control. Mom insists it's the first time in months and she just slipped. She's remorseful."

"Did you talk to her?" she asked.

"I did. She agreed to the rehab and you know she doesn't do that. This is all part of the process. I'm going to get her and drop her off there now."

"I'm going with you," she said.

"You don't need to," Liz said.

"Yeah, I do. Sorry they woke you up."

"Don't worry about it," Liz said. "When can you get out of work?"

"I'll leave now and go to your house and we'll take Mom. Thanks for setting it up."

"See you soon," Liz said and hung up.

Abby's eyes filled with tears. It always seemed when she got her hopes up these things happened. She didn't know why she couldn't accept it like Liz and guard her heart more.

31

PUSHING OFF THE ENVIABLE

West hadn't talked to Abby much the past few days. He wasn't sure what was going on, but she was more distant than normal.

He didn't want to think it was his work that was crazy since it was normal for him to be working as early as seven and as late as eight.

The fact that all the news of his relationship had died down and life seemed to be steady again should be a good thing, but he felt like that might not be the case with his girlfriend.

Abby hadn't even commented about if she was coming or not this weekend. He knew that he shouldn't be pushing it weekly again, but he just wanted to see her.

He figured he was more accepting of the travel even though she'd said before it was too much for her.

Maybe he would go to her. He'd call her soon and they'd figure it out.

He finished with the last of the emails for now. He'd been home for an hour and he figured Abby would be in for the night. It was past seven and she was probably watching TV.

He called, but she didn't answer. Hmm. That wasn't like her.

Rather than leave a voicemail, he sent her a text. She'd call when she had a chance.

He should know by now that she didn't always jump when he called even if he was getting used to her trying to answer when he did.

Thirty minutes later, his phone rang, he saw it was Abby and answered. "Hi," he said. "You busy?"

"I was out running errands," she said.

"Oh. No problem. I didn't tell you I was calling. We haven't talked much lately and I thought I'd see what was going on."

There was silence on the other end. "West. We need to talk."

"We are," he said, laughing.

"No," she said. "About us."

He felt his heart thumping in his chest. "What's wrong?"

"I don't think this is working out."

"What isn't? I'll try to come to you this weekend. Let me look at my schedule."

"You don't like coming here because we have to stay in a hotel. You don't like my bed and it's not big enough. I get it. But I don't need you to send me a new one."

He'd offered more than once. He was just going to do it one day and Laken told him not to even consider it if Abby had told him no.

"I can stay there," he said.

"No," she said. "I'm just running nonstop. I miss you when I'm not with you, but when I'm there you're stressed or sneaking away to do work when you think I don't know."

He'd done that a few times. Gotten up in the middle of the night when she was sleeping to take care of things. Or up earlier than her. He didn't think she'd know or mind. Guess he was wrong.

"I'll pay more attention to you," he argued.

"I don't want you to do something you can't or don't want to do. I know your career comes first. I know you support a ton of people, not just your family. You can't stand failure."

He couldn't, yet here it was looking like the one relationship he'd had in his adult life was going to crumble.

"I can't," he said. "Don't do this. We can figure it out. You can move here and we'll see more of each other. If you want to work, fine, if not, then don't. Stay at the Hamptons and just relax. I can fly back and forth or split my time from there to Manhattan."

She laughed on the other end. Not a happy sound like he would have hoped. "Don't you get it? You just told me what to do. You didn't ask what I wanted. We don't talk it out. Hardly ever. You tell me all the time how to handle things and give me options but never ask if I even want one of them. You're used to calling the shots."

Shit. "I can't break a lifetime of that," he said. "I'm trying."

"I know. I appreciate it. Maybe things could have been different if I was closer, but I'm not. An hour flight is still a few hours of traveling between airports and homes. We've been doing this for months. In my mind I had hoped it'd work, but maybe I just knew all along it'd be too much. I let you convince me to give it a try."

"It was working," he said, trying not to sound as desperate as he was feeling. "You know it. I'm not sure what changed. Don't tell me it's the articles that were released. It blew over fast just as I said it would. You handled it so well."

"That has nothing to do with it," she argued. "I feel like I'm just pushing off the inevitable. It's probably best to cut it off now before it gets any deeper."

"Really?" he asked. "You love me. I love you. How much deeper are we talking?"

He couldn't believe this was happening and that he'd felt so blindsided by it.

Why didn't he see it?

How could he see it though if he didn't see or talk to her much?

"Sometimes love just isn't enough," she said softly.

"You're crying," he said. "I hear it in your voice."

Probably because he knew his own voice was shaking and his eyes were itching. He wasn't sure the last time he cried. Probably when he found out his father had died.

"Because I'm sad," she said.

"You don't need to be," he said. "We can work this out."

"We can't," she said. "To work it out means I've got to bend even more. It's my life changing, not yours. I'm not sure you can see that. Or even appreciate it. At least it doesn't feel that way."

He was taken aback by those truthful words.

Nothing in his life changed other than every few weeks he flew to see her and came back.

Even when he spent time with her in the Hamptons, he was working.

He had people he paid to clean and take care of everything not work related. He even had a team of people under him dealing with those things.

For Abby, she was one person who was stubborn and never wanted anything from him. Maybe he didn't ask because he didn't like to be told no. That was on him and he knew it.

The only thing he'd been able to give her were the earrings and that was because he'd left them in her luggage without her knowledge.

He felt like an idiot for not seeing these things.

"I do appreciate it," he said. "I appreciate you. I love you."

"Don't make this harder than it is," she said, crying now.

He wasn't going to beg and he was getting damn close to it.

He had his pride.

"So this is it?" he said. "We're done?"

"I'm not sure what else to do. I'm sorry, West. I do love you. Just remember that. I never meant to hurt you."

"Bye, Abby," he said and hung up.

What more could he say? She wasn't going to listen and had made up her mind.

He tossed his phone down on his desk at his penthouse and sat back.

It wasn't until he saw the drops hit his desk that he realized he was crying and that somehow he'd lost the best thing that happened in his life and didn't know one way to fix it.

Wanting it badly just wasn't enough.

32

LOVE HURTS

"How are you doing?" Abby's father asked her two days later. Normally she'd be flying to see West at this point on a Friday, but since she'd ended things, she was home.

Her father knew what was going on. She'd told Liz what she'd done, her sister telling her that she was making a mistake but couldn't talk her out of it. Liz then told her father, who called and wanted her to come to dinner.

"I'm fine," she said.

Her voice shook a bit. She wasn't fine but knew she made the right decision.

"Then why are you upset if you're fine?" her father asked. He was standing at the grill on the deck and flipping burgers. She tried not to think of West and how he must have paid through the nose to get burgers when they were in Aruba.

He never thought much of things like that.

If he wanted it, he bought it.

She couldn't be something that was bought even though enough people had said it to her lately.

Everyone at work was always asking about the fun things they did together, the private jet and what West was buying her.

She always told them nothing. Other than the jet, it was the only thing that they did.

No fancy trips or restaurants. Even when they went out it wasn't anything outrageous. It's like he tried to keep it low-key for her.

She didn't want him doing that though. She wanted him to do what he was used to, not changing who he was because of her.

Which of course just contradicted what she'd said to him. That nothing changed for him but everything was for her.

Making concessions about restaurants didn't count in her eyes.

"Because it hurts," she said. "Love hurts. You've said that before. I saw it with you and Mom. You still loved her but finally had to let her go."

"That's different and you know it," her father said. "I tried for years. You can't help someone who doesn't want to be helped. You saw that recently. Please don't tell me you ended things with West because of what your mother did."

She sniffled some more. "No."

"Abby," her father said firmly. "Don't lie to me. And remember, I know you well enough to know when you are."

Her eyes were looking at her feet. She always looked down when she lied.

"Dad. It's not going to work out. I know it. I've known it all along and don't know why I tried to think it could. It's just saving me more heartache in the future."

"If you can predict the future, then tell me the lotto numbers tonight. Maybe I can retire early."

"Not funny," she said.

"No," her father said. "It's not. It's never been funny. Your whole life you've worn your heart on your sleeve. You've been disappointed more times than I can count by your mother's actions. We've tried to warn you, but you can only tell someone so many times."

"I can't help it," she said. "It hurts."

"I know you think Liz is hard by not letting your mother in. She lets her in, what she doesn't do is let it bring her down. It took me years to get there. Don't take it out on West for what your mother did. It kills me to see you hurting like this. It's a father's job to protect their children and I didn't do that great of a job at it."

"Don't do that, Dad. You're the best. This is on me. You've warned me enough."

"There is no one to blame. I don't like seeing you hurt. How did West take it? Something tells me he's not a man that likes to be told no."

It was the dry tone her father used. Not in an insult but more like ironic. "He was upset. I mean it seemed it to me. He told me to move there and I didn't have to work. Or I could find a job. He didn't care."

"He told you that," her father said.

"Yes," she said. *Told me*. Didn't ask. Just said do it. He didn't ask what I wanted. He never does."

"Maybe it was a figure of speech more than anything," her father said.

"I don't know. Why aren't you saying anything about that? What if I said yes?"

"Abby," her father said. "I can see how much you love West. I'd never keep you back. I didn't keep Liz from moving away. She knew enough to come home when she needed it. Though I wish I'd known earlier what was going on in her life, I had to resign myself to the fact that she knew I'd be there for her. Just like you know I will be too. Besides, it's not like I thought you'd stay here if you continued to date him, but you go back and forth enough, that I could do the same."

Her father never talked to her about this.

"You could have," she said.

Her father just lifted an eyebrow at her. "So West seemed upset and nothing more?"

She shrugged. "I haven't talked to him since he hung up on me."

Her bottom lip was wobbling more now and she couldn't hold the tears back and just put her head down and cried.

Most men ran when a woman cried around them. Her father just walked through the house, grabbed the box of tissues and put them in front of her. He was used to this though she hadn't done it in years.

Her teen years were much more emotional while she waited time and again for her mother to come home.

When she moved out, no one saw the tears she had.

"That wasn't nice of him to hang up."

"He said bye and then hung up. I don't know what I expected. It's better this way. A clean cut."

No matter how much she told herself this was for the best, it still hurt.

She supposed she should be happy he was listening to her when she thought at times he'd heard her.

She had nothing more to do other than think the past few days and everything she came up with was how much West had been trying to make her feel comfortable.

How he put her first even when she met his family.

She never once felt out of place around him or his siblings.

Not true. She did when she was at his penthouse that first time. But the second time was easier.

It got easier each time.

Maybe she did let what happened with her mother cause her to overreact.

The fear of being left by him in the future made her cut the strings first rather than find her voice and talk to him. She could have brought any topic up with him at any time and yet she always told herself he'd be busy or not have time for her.

Not that he'd know that. He had no clue what happened this week with her family because she hadn't told him.

The hardest thing she had to do was let Aileen know she'd ended things with West this morning.

She hadn't talked to Aileen in a few days. It just told her West didn't tell his siblings or his mother what was going on.

Why would he? It was only two days ago. She knew he was a private person.

Could be he was trying to figure out what to say.

Again, he hated to fail, she knew that. He'd see this as a failure.

"It doesn't look better from where I'm standing," her father said. "You had something you always wanted and threw it away because it's not lining up the way you thought it should in your head. Eat up."

That was her father's way of getting his point across and not saying anymore.

He'd put the burger on a bun and then on a plate for her. She reached for the bag of chips that he'd opened and took some of them out too.

The first bite went down hard, then the next one got better.

Life was going to go on and she'd have to find a way to do it alone because she wasn't sure she'd find another man she could love as much as West, but she'd made her decision and he wasn't the type that would give her another chance now that she realized what a stupid mistake she'd made.

33

ALL MAKES SENSE

"When were you going to tell me that Abby broke up with you?" his mother said the minute he answered the phone on Friday.

It was five and most were leaving for the day in his office. He'd stay as long as he wanted because it's not like he had anywhere to be or someone to see.

"Guess you found out from her," he said. It was the only way his mother could have. He hadn't told a soul.

He didn't even want to think about the fact that Abby wouldn't be in his life anymore let alone that she ended things with him.

"Don't take that tone with me," his mother said. "It's not like she texted to tell me. Your sister said you've been a bear the last few days when I talked to her yesterday."

"She's used to it," he said.

"She was used to it before Abby. She didn't know if something was going on. I talked to Braylon. It's like pulling teeth to get him to say anything, but he didn't argue that you've been an ass. I texted Abby to check in with her and she told me. Now it all makes sense. What did you do?"

"Beats the hell out of me," he said. He figured he might as well talk to her or she'd bug him. Maybe if he gave her enough she'd leave him alone and tell the rest of the family for him too.

"Okay, then what didn't you do for her?" his mother asked.

"Beats the hell out of me there too. She said she can't do this anymore. It's too much going back and forth."

"Of course it is," his mother said. "I'm surprised she's doing it as much as she is. Between her job, her family, planning her sister's wedding, what happened to her mother this week. She needs a break and running to spend time with you is probably only adding to it. I thought she told you before it was too much and yet you got back into the weekly swing again."

"What happened to her mother?" he asked. He ignored the fact that his mother pointed out something he realized too. That Abby did tell him it was too much but yet each week they talked about plans and she never said she didn't want to or couldn't come.

"You don't know?" his mother said.

"No," he said. "She hardly ever talks about her mother or father. Not even the wedding plans." He knew the wedding was in November. He'd marked his calendar so that he'd make sure he could be there for it. Guess it didn't matter now.

"Maybe because you don't ask," his mother said. "Didn't Talia and I tell you that back in July? That you don't find things out unless you ask."

"It's intrusive," he argued.

"Not to the woman you love," his mother said. "But maybe you don't love her like I thought you did."

He was going to ignore his mother's comment. "Her mother. What happened?"

"I guess Lily is back in rehab. She signed out over the weekend and didn't return when she should have. When she came back they drug tested her. Liz and Abby put her back in rehab right away. I'm sure it's not easy to get your hopes up for something for months and then have them squashed again."

"I don't know why she wouldn't have told me this," he said.

"Because she probably didn't want to burden you with it," his mother said. "And *you don't ask* her things."

Guilty. "I told her to move here," he said. "If she lived closer we'd see each other more. She wouldn't have all those stresses like she's got."

His mother laughed. "You *told* her."

Fuck. "Yes."

"Again," his mother said, "she isn't an employee. She's your girlfriend. You ask. You don't tell. Didn't you tell me before that she didn't jump when you wanted her to? That you liked that."

"Yes," he said.

"Yet you are still treating her like you do everyone else other than family. She deserves some respect. She may be younger than you, but she has a voice. You need to listen to it more."

He wished he'd been told all of this before Wednesday.

"She made her choice," he said. "I heard her."

"You're an idiot," his mother said.

"Thanks, Mom. Love you too."

His mother laughed. "West. I'm not going to tell you what to do."

"Why?" he said. "You do it all the time."

"This time you have to figure it out on your own. Push your pride aside and reach out to her one more time. Find out if it's really over or if maybe you could work it out. Don't ask if she overreacted. Don't tell her to do something. Ask her what you could do *for her*. What you could do to make it easier that has nothing to do with money. If she has no answers. If she's still done, then you know you did what you could."

"And what if I'm just setting myself up to be knocked down again?" he asked.

"Then it only humbles you like the rest of the men in the world. Get over yourself. When you love someone enough, you make that step. If you don't love her, then just go back to being the person you were before Abby entered your life. I was getting used to you being like you were before your father died. I thought you liked it yourself."

His mother hung up on him after that. Nothing like an epic mic drop to put him in his place.

He made some calls, then grabbed his phone and laptop to get to the roof to catch a helicopter ride to the airport.

He'd surprised her once and it worked. He was hoping he could again.

It was almost nine when he was finally knocking on her door. He'd seen her car in the parking lot so knew she was home.

Her expression was almost comical when she opened the door.

"Give me thirty minutes of your time. That's all I ask. Then if you still say we are done, I'll have to accept it. No. *Can* I have thirty minutes of your time?"

She kept blinking her eyes at him. When the tears filled and overran he wasn't sure if that was good or bad.

But when the words came out of her mouth, he knew he had a chance. "As opposed to thirty days to form a habit."

"Something like that," he said.

She moved aside to let him in. "I want to say I'm surprised you're here."

"But you're not," he said. "Maybe you were hoping I'd come to you?"

She started to cry even more and nodded her head but the smile filled her face. "I've missed you."

This was going better than he thought, but he was still going to follow his mother's advice. It was the right thing to do.

"I've missed you too. Why didn't you tell me about your mother?"

She grabbed a tissue and blew her nose. When she was done he went and pulled her into his arms. He had to hold her again. It felt like years rather than just a week.

"You're busy," she said. "You don't need to be bothered with my problems."

He hated that she felt that way. "People in love talk about what is going on in their life. I'm at fault for not asking more. I should have. I will do it in the future."

She nodded again. The fact she didn't argue it told him how wrong he was, but made him hopeful at the same time. "I know you've got a lot going on."

"Which doesn't excuse me taking an active interest in your life. You always ask about me and what is going on. My family too. I know you talk to my mother. Yet you don't say much about your personal life."

"It's boring to you," she said.

"No," he said, hugging her tighter. "It's not. I'm sorry you feel that way. I'm sorry that I ever made you feel that way and I should have seen it myself and am mad I didn't."

"Your mother told you, didn't she?" she asked.

He leaned back and kissed her on the lips. "She did. She said a lot of things to me. Lectured me good and will kick my butt if I make a mistake like this in the future."

She smiled. "I love your mother. She's everything I always wanted in life. Or wanted my mother to be."

He hated that he didn't know that either. That she didn't feel she could open up enough to tell him those things.

"Abby, I know you have trust issues. I should have remembered all of that. I guess I got ahead of myself and felt like I won you over."

She raised her eyebrows. "You don't own me."

"I know," he said, his hand going up. "Let me finish, please. I shouldn't have just assumed things were fine after those thirty days. I should have put more effort in. I should have talked more, asked more. Everything. I worried so much that this would all be too much for you and I tried to help that way rather than focusing on the right things to do and say."

"I know you mean well. Or meant well. I don't need to be bought. I've told you that before."

"And I haven't tried to do that either. You've slapped my hand enough."

"It's not about money."

"No," he said. "It's about respecting that you are your own person. That you can make your decisions and you have a voice."

"Sounds like something your mother said to you," she said with her head tilted.

"She's not wrong," he said. "And trust me when I say I know I've been wrong a lot."

"We all have been. Myself included. I shouldn't have

done what I had on Wednesday. Liz told me to give it time before I made a decision."

Which meant she talked to her sister but not him. "Let me ask you this. Just answer with your heart. Do you want to end things with me? Don't think about all the ways it won't work. Just answer that."

"No, I don't. It hurts so much. I worried that it'd hurt more later on when it happened."

"No one says it's going to happen."

"As my father told me tonight. He said if I could read into the future I should give him the lotto numbers."

West smiled. "I knew I liked your father."

"He likes you," she said. "He really does. He told me I was a fool for what I did based on what happened with my mother this week."

"So it was that," he said. "She let you down once again and you feared that I would do it too? That I was already. That maybe you'd take control of the situation rather than wait for it to happen to you again?"

"Yes," she said. "Stupid, I know. Then I thought you'd never take me back and I had to live with what I'd done."

Which meant she wanted to be with him.

"*You* tell me what you need from me. I can ask you and I am. But you have to talk to me too. I want this to work. I love you. I don't want to lose you. If we talk we can figure this out. I have to be more open and so do you."

"I don't know what I want or need. That's the problem. You live there and I live here."

"Do you have to live here?" he asked. "Do you want to live with me? Do you want a house here and I try to split my time that way between here and Manhattan? I guess when it comes down to it, the time in the air is about the same."

He didn't know why he didn't think of that.

"No," she said. "It's not the same and you know it. What I want is to be with you. I don't have an answer for you today, but I'd like to try to figure it out. Together. I don't want to be taken care of. I'd go nuts if I didn't work and sat around all day long doing nothing."

"There is no reason for you to go nuts. I also know that you don't want to work in Manhattan. You don't want to live there either."

"It's not as horrible as I thought it'd be."

"To visit," he said, laughing. "I know. It's why I've got the house in the Hamptons and went there on the weekends. I needed to escape just as much. I don't want to go back there alone. But it's not about what I want, it's about what you want."

"I want you," she said. "If you'll have me back after what I did."

"You know I will," he said. "In my heart, I never let you go. I don't ever want to."

"Neither do I," she said, kissing him. "How about we get a hotel for the night?"

"Or we can stay here. The less room in your bed, the more I get to hold you."

"We can do that too," she said, taking his hand and pulling him to her room. "And tomorrow we can see about fitting a king-sized bed in here for you."

"Anything you want," he said. "It's yours."

"I only want you," she said.

EPILOGUE

T*hree Months Later*

"THAT WAS A NICE WEDDING," West said to Abby. Liz and Christian were married and had left for their honeymoon.

The wedding was beautiful and her mother even looked lovely. She was back on the right track again and Abby could only hope it continued, but she knew enough to accept it was still a long road.

She and West were now on his jet flying to his home in the Hamptons.

She'd spent Thanksgiving with his family and it was the biggest loudest holiday she'd had in her life.

She loved every single minute of it.

They flew home Friday morning and got ready for the rehearsal dinner, everyone meeting West for the first time, though it was no secret who she was dating.

Thankfully, very few knew she'd broken up with West for forty-eight hours.

"It was," she said. "Liz looked beautiful. Happier than she was when she walked down the aisle the first time. I guess it just goes to show when you know the person is right for you."

She turned and put her head on his shoulder. They were sitting on the big sectional in front of the TV, though it wasn't on. She liked how it almost felt as if they were in a living room and not on a plane.

"I'm glad you feel that way," he said. "And things are going well for you too? With us?"

"Yes," she said, laughing.

He asked her pretty much weekly. He'd even been so attentive about her life and job. Sometimes he asked too many questions and she started laughing at him, but she appreciated that he was trying.

They were only spending every other weekend with each other now. She'd take Thursday and Friday off and spend the four days with him in the Hamptons. He'd fly in Friday afternoon and stay at her place. With her king-sized bed.

Though they were spending less time together, they were talking more during the week. Having real conversations.

Not once had he brought up her moving there and she knew he was giving her time to make that decision on her own.

"And you'll tell me otherwise?" he asked.

"I will. There is one thing I wanted to talk to you about," she said.

"Tell me," he said.

"I've been thinking. Maybe it's time to talk about my future."

"Okay," he said. "What is it that you want or are thinking of?"

Asking her again. "That I'd like to maybe give it a try living with you. Moving in with you. I've been looking for jobs and seeing what might be available. No one stays at their first company their whole career. I've been there over six years."

She'd put a lot of thought into it. She wasn't out to conquer the HR world. She didn't want to be a big boss or director. But she'd like to do more and where she was, she was limited.

"I'd love to have you move in with me," he said. "Just say the word and we'll get you packed up while you take your time and figure out what you want to do while you're there. Work or not. You can work for me too."

"I think too many people would talk," she said.

"I don't care," he said. "If you want to work for me, we can find a place for you. Actually, I hadn't wanted to bring this up, but Laken needs someone. Someone that will deal with all those policies and procedures and any other HR issues with new acquisitions and existing businesses that she oversees."

"Really?" she asked.

"Yes. She brought it up a few weeks ago. You two get along well. You can work out logistics, but she's hardly ever in the office. It's not like I think you'd need to be there. Again, whatever you want."

"It's coming from Laken and not you?" she asked.

"I swear it is," he said. "You can ask her yourself."

"She might not want me though," she said.

"Trust me, she'd be thrilled. I mean it. You heard her at

Thanksgiving when you were talking about your job and everything you did and that she wished you worked for her."

She'd just thought that was Laken being nice. Maybe she was wrong.

"I'll think about it," she said. "One step at a time. If you're okay with the move, then I'd like to start planning."

"I'm more than okay," he said. "I know you overheard me saying something about this months ago but never said anything to me about it. Why?"

"Because it was too early," she said. "And when it did come up, you didn't ask. You just almost ordered it."

"And we know I won't do that again," he said, rubbing her shoulder.

"No," she said, giggling.

"I know this is probably too soon. I just can't wait," he said. "And the fact you are bringing up living with me seems like the perfect timing."

She frowned and watched him get up and walk away from her and go into his room, then come back out.

Before she could say anything, he got down on his knee in front of her. "Oh my God."

"Abby. I love you. You know it. You've changed me and how I view the world. You've made me realize the person I was as a kid could still be there as an adult. Money doesn't change that."

She was shaking her head no at his words. "I fell in love with the man I met in Aruba. Not the billionaire you turned out to be."

He flipped the lid on the box in front of him. She wasn't shocked to see the massive diamond ring staring at her. It had to be easily a three-carat teardrop surrounded by more diamonds on a thick band. "I'm asking you to be my wife. To love me until the day I die. To wear this ring and be reminded of the tears I shed when I thought you weren't going to be in my life anymore."

It was the first time he'd said he'd cried when she ended things for those stupid two days.

"Yes," she said. "It will be a reminder of my tears when I thought I threw it all away. No more."

He took the ring out of the box and slid it on her finger. "I wanted to go bigger. Your father told me if I did you wouldn't wear it. This was the compromise."

"My father knows?" she asked, smiling.

"I had to ask his permission," he said. "It's the right thing to do."

She launched herself forward and hugged him.

"We know you always do the right thing," she said. "Even saving me from being hit on in a bar."

"Best pickup line of my life," he said.

Her jaw dropped. "What?"

"Joking," he said.

"Are you?"

"Yes. Or am I?" he asked, flipping her on her back and kissing the shocked look off her face.

She'd ask him again later. When she wasn't busy.

For now, it didn't matter.

Nothing did other than she was finally going to open herself up fully and throw away all her trust issues.

Guess when you found the right person, anything was possible.

THE END!

.   .   .

CHECK out the next in the series, Love To The Rescue

PROLOGUE

"Are you sure about this, Lily?" She gave her older sister a one-eyed squint. "Lilian," Quinn said. "I'm sorry. I've known you as Lily for over twenty-four years. It's hard to start calling you Lilian now."

"It's more professional sounding," Lilian said. She supposed for years it was fine to be Lily, but now she was moving to the Big Apple.

She wanted to make something of herself.

She wanted a job where she would be respected and looked at as someone knowledgeable. Someone not raised in the foster care system with a mother in and out of jail and a father whose name she didn't even know.

"I'm nervous for you," Quinn said. Quinn was ten years older than her and married to a plastic surgeon. The same single father who'd hired her older sister to be his nanny years ago in Lake Placid.

"Don't be," she said. "You never really cared for the bigger city living. I liked it. I gave this a try, but there just isn't room for growth here."

Quinn sighed. "I know. I've loved having you so close for the past six years. I really have."

"I've loved being here," Lilian said.

She'd never be able to thank her sister enough for taking her in when she graduated high school in Chicago.

Her foster parents let her stay past eighteen so that she could finish up high school. They were great and would try to help her as best they could, but after graduation she knew she'd be on her own. Though she got a lot of financial aid for college, it was living somewhere during breaks that would be hard. As wonderful as the Websters were, they needed her spot for another child to help.

Her brother-in-law opened the doors to his beautiful home on the lake for her and let her stay in the housekeeper quarters that Quinn had first lived in.

Lily had to admit, it was the nicest house she'd ever seen, let alone lived in. She went to college in Plattsburg an hour away, lived in the dorms and had a place to come home to when she wanted.

Her first job out of college wasn't exactly her dream career in communication and she knew the chances of finding something she wanted were slim to none in this area.

But she'd been making it work for two years while living with her sister, helping her out with Max's older kids, Davy and Lara, and Quinn and Max's two kids, Jocelyn and Carson.

It was time for her to move on though. Or at least to start trying.

Finding a job and then a place to live wasn't going to be easy, but nothing in her life had ever been easy.

"We loved having you. I hope you don't think you're in the way. No one thinks that. You have your own little apartment in the back. You've got friends and a life here. You're hardly in the way."

She saw Quinn's eyes fill a little with tears.

"I don't feel that way. You've got everything under control like you always did. Davy is going off to college soon."

"It's so hard to believe he's a senior and graduating in six months. I think Max is going to struggle there."

"He probably will," she said. "But he's got Lara to keep

him on his toes for two more years, and then the start of everything all over again with Jocelyn and Carson."

Her niece was in kindergarten, her nephew was only three.

"I'm going to miss you," Quinn said.

"You're making it sound like I'm leaving tomorrow," she said, laughing. "I'm just telling you that I've decided to look for a job and then a place to stay. I'm not sure what is going to be harder. Probably a place to stay."

"It's going to be so expensive there," Quinn said.

"I've got a lot of money put away because you and Max don't let me pay for anything. Which I appreciate. You taught me how to budget. I'll be fine."

She'd never had much growing up. Like Quinn, what she had and earned she held onto as tightly as getting the squeeze from an octopus. It'd help her when the time was right.

"I know you will," Quinn said. "I'm worrying over nothing. You've got a good head on your shoulders and you always have. Tess and Ronnie did such a good job with you."

"You did a good job with me," she said, hugging her sister. "I know how much you wanted to take me in and you beat yourself up over it for years."

Quinn had desperately wanted to raise her siblings, but it would have never happened. Working two to three jobs and moving around as much as she was, she'd never get custody. She could barely care for herself, and having three younger kids with her without the means for childcare wouldn't have worked.

"I did," Quinn said. "But Max told me to let it go. I did the best I could and things happen for a reason. You're going to be fine. Brett is hanging in there with Annie and his kids. Karl, well, he's trying."

"No one blames you for anything," she said. "Just remember that. We thank you all the time for the help you've given us."

Lilian knew that Quinn helped her two brothers out for years too. In some aspects, she was luckier than a lot of people with her past.

"I don't want thanks. I just want everyone happy."

"And I am," Lily said. "I'll be even happier when I can find a career that I've been dreaming of. It will happen, but it's not meant to happen here."

"No," Quinn said. "I selfishly wanted you to stay, but I knew at some point I'd have to let you go. You won't be far and Max's parents will be close by if you need anything. They expect you to stay in touch."

She sighed. It was the last thing she wanted to do, but she would if she had no choice in the matter.

"I will," she said. "Now let me help you with dinner. The kids will be home soon with Max."

Max had taken them skiing for the day. All but Carson who was taking his afternoon nap.

"That I will let you do," Quinn said. "I'm going to soak it all up while I can because I know you're going to find exactly what you're looking for and it will be soon."

"I hope you're right," she said, laughing.

Chapter One
Too Good To Be True

Eight Months Later

Lilian wasn't thinking anything about that conversation with her sister, Quinn, eight months later as she got ready for work in her little four-hundred-square-foot studio apartment that she could barely afford. Living on yogurt and ramen noodles helped. So did walking the six blocks to work each day saving her any transportation costs. Come winter though, she wasn't so sure that was going to be an option on the really cold days.

She'd deal with it then. The three months she'd lived here had been somewhat wonderful.

Not the job part that turned out to be too good to be true.

Yep, she was putting her communication degree to work. Little did she know being an Assistant Communications Manager actually meant being an *assistant* to the Communications Manager. Who was still notches under the Communications Director and the VP of Communications. There were others in between, but she'd lost track at this point.

So the truth was she spent most of her time running errands, taking notes, assisting in writing policies and procedures for the insurance firm she worked for and getting all the grunt work handed over.

In her mind, it was nothing more than what an intern would do.

But the salary drew her in and she found it just cost so much more to live here that of course the salary would be higher.

She was considering a second job on the weekends because during the week was out of the question with her having to work late all the time with no notice.

Lilian finished with her makeup in the small bathroom, packed up her supplies in the little cosmetic bag and put it under the sink. There was no room to leave anything on the counter more than her toothbrush.

She walked over behind the wardrobe unit that held her clothing, shoes, towels, pantry items and even spare sheets and blankets. That was the only thing separating her bed from the couch and the TV she had on the wall.

She found the shoes she wanted to wear in the bin where they were all neatly stored. It was the only way everything fit.

Her bed was made, the doors were shut on the unit and she moved to the living room to check everything was picked up there. The last thing she wanted to do was come home to clutter.

She packed her lunch in the little galley kitchen, then grabbed her laptop and purse and walked out the door. No elevator in her building, so she went down the two flights of stairs.

Ten minutes later, she was turning the corner in downtown Manhattan toward the high-rise building she worked in, and pulling the fake diamond out of her purse and slipping it on her finger. There was a little coffee shop she had to stop at today like she did every Monday and get her boss and staff members their coffee. They allowed her to get one for herself too. Yay her. It was her splurge of the week.

She put her order in and went to sit off to the side while she waited. One of the drinks was always complicated and took forever. She felt like a fool even giving it and had to read it off the text they all sent her the night before. Some texted her this morning, but they knew it had to be before seven as she was getting the order to be in her office by seven thirty.

"There you are again."

She turned and held back her sigh. For over a month

now, the server would come and talk to her while he dropped off orders. Flirt with her was more like it.

"I'm here," she said.

"You look nice."

"Thanks," she said. Lilian never addressed him by his name though she knew it. It was even on his nametag.

It was rude, but she didn't want to give any indication that she was interested.

Connor was his name. He'd asked her out twice, and twice she'd said no. But he'd kept up the flirting even after she'd shown up with the ring on. His eyes had landed on it, but he never asked another question about it.

"I should get to work," Connor said.

"Yeah, you should," another man said. His name was Rod. He was a dick.

He was always talking down to the employees while he got his skinny latte.

The first time she'd heard that order she wanted to laugh but didn't. That wouldn't be nice.

He also had asked her out. Three times. She told him no. Every. Single. Time.

It drove her insane that she appeared to be fresh blood in the ocean around a pool of sharks when she'd first walked in the door of the cafe months ago.

By now, most of the men who came here knew she was a regular and when she showed up they circled her like flies on melted ice cream.

She turned back to her phone and hoped Rod would go to another seat. He didn't.

He came and sat across from her. "Is there something you want?" she asked.

Lilian didn't want to come off as a bitch, but she could

handle herself. She had spent so much of her life trying to blend in and not be noticed.

She wasn't sure why it wasn't working here.

"I'm curious why you never talk about your fiancé," Rod said.

"I don't normally talk to anyone while I'm here," she said. "I'm just getting coffee for work and then getting on with my day."

"I've asked about you, Lilian Baker."

Her face color drained a bit. "Who have you asked and why?" She never gave her last name here. Only her first. Rod was not a coworker, only someone she saw here at the cafe.

"Just trying to find out more about you. I've heard your name given when you've come in here. Your work badge was exposed out of your purse one day."

She'd have to be more careful. Her sister would throw a fit if she knew that.

"That's a little intrusive," she said, angling her head. She was a bit more sarcastic than she wanted to be, but it was hard not to put her foot down.

He laughed at her. Like he thought she was flirting with him. As if she'd be *flattered* he'd done what he had.

"Nah," Rod said. "Just letting you know. You know what I think?"

"I'm sure you're going to tell me," she said, putting her phone down.

He smirked. "I think that ring is fake. I think either your fiancé is trying to pull one over on you...or you don't have a fiancé at all. You're too young to have a ring that big. Unless of course you're dating an older man."

She shouldn't have bought this ring, but it looked pretty online and as real as she could get. It was two carats. It was just a single stone and it looked fine to her. It's not like she wore it anywhere other than in this coffee shop and to work.

She hadn't meant to wear it in the office, but she'd forgotten to take it off one day.

Of course, one of her coworkers saw it and asked.

The ring also hadn't stopped one of the other managers that she didn't work with from making inappropriate comments to her about her attire.

Well, not necessarily inappropriate but unwanted, and saying no didn't seem to stop it either.

Now she had to keep the ring on or someone would ask where it went. She almost admitted why she had it on one day but was glad she didn't if Rod was asking about her.

If he knew where she worked, he might know someone in the building. For all she knew, he worked in the building too. There were more businesses in there than she knew of.

"Does it matter?" she asked. "It's none of your business."

Rod shrugged. "It could be there is no fiancé or even any boyfriend at all."

He was smirking at her now.

"Hey, honey," she heard and turned her head to see a gorgeous guy in a suit standing next to her. "You left before me this morning. I thought we were going to leave at the same time."

Rod's jaw dropped and she wasn't sure why. All she could think of was she couldn't get away from this crap, but the guy in the suit had been in here before. He always watched and didn't say much to anyone.

He was often on his phone, as she was. Sometimes he was talking to people, but she tried not to listen. It was rude.

And right now, the look in his eye told her he was trying to help.

Maybe if she just played along all this attention on her

would end once and for all. If she had her way, she'd just find another coffee shop, but it wasn't her choice.

"Sorry about that," she said. "You were running late and you know I have a meeting this morning."

The guy laughed. He had his drink in his hand. Looked to be just a normal coffee like she got.

Her drinks were being brought over saving her once again. Or so she thought until the mystery man said, "Then let's walk out together."

Lilian hoped he didn't turn out to be another guy hitting on her, but she didn't have much of a choice unless she wanted her ruse discovered, so she stood and let the sexy man put his hand on her lower back to shift her out of the way as he lifted the drink tray off the table for her.

There were a lot of eyes on her when she walked out and she had no idea why that was. Her best hope was she could convince her coworkers that they needed to get coffee from another place. Maybe she could spike one of them to give someone a stomachache and that would help her cause?!

ALSO BY NATALIE ANN

Trevor Miles and Riley Hamilton – Last Chance

Matt Winters and Dena Hall- Another Chance

Logan Taylor and Kennedy Miles- It's My Chance

Justin Cambridge and Taryn Miles – One More Chance

The Fierce Five Series

Gavin Fierce and Jolene O'Malley- How Gavin Stole Christmas

Brody Fierce and Aimee Reed - Brody

Aiden Fierce and Nic Moretti- Aiden

Mason Fierce and Jessica Corning- Mason

Cade Fierce and Alex Marshall - Cade

Ella Fierce and Travis McKinley- Ella

Fierce Family

Sam Fierce and Dani Rhodes- Sam

Bryce Fierce and Payton Davies - Bryce

Drake Fierce and Kara Winslow – Drake

Noah Fierce and Paige Parker - Noah

Wyatt Fierce and Adriana Lopez – Wyatt

Jade Fierce and Brock James – Jade

Ryder Fierce and Marissa McMillan – Ryder

Fierce Matchmaking

Devin Andrews and Hope Hall- Devin

Mick McNamara and Lindsey White- Mick

Cody McMillian and Raina Davenport – Cody

Liam O'Malley and Margo West- Liam

Walker Olson and Stella White – Walker

Flynn Slater and Julia McNamara – Flynn

Ivan Andrews & Kendra Key- Ivan

Jonah Davenport & Megan Harrington- Jonah

Royce Kennedy & Chloe Grey- Royce

Sawyer Brennan & Faith O'Malley- Sawyer

Trent Davenport & Roni Hollister- Trent

Gabe McCarthy & Elise Kennedy – Gabe

Ben Kelley & Eve Hall – Ben

Paradise Place

Josh Turner and Ruby Gentile – Cupid's Quest

Harris Walker and Kaelyn Butler – Change Up

Philip Aire and Blair McKay- Starting Over

Nathan Randal and Brina Shepard – Eternal

Ryan Butler and Shannon Wilder – Falling Into Love

Brian Dawson and Robin Masters – Mistletoe Magic

Caden Finley and Sarah Walker- Believe In Me

Evan Butler and Parker Reed – Unexpected Delivery

Trey Bridges and Whitney Butler – Forever Mine

Dylan Randal and Zoe Milton- Because Of You

Cash Fielding and Hannah Shepard – Letting Go

Brent Elliot and Vivian Getman – No More Hiding

Marcus Reid and Addison Fielding- Made For Me

Rick Masters and Gillian Bridges – The One

Cooper Winslow and Morgan Finely- Back To Me

Jeremy Reid and McKenna Preston- Saving Me

Christian Butler and Liz Carter- Begin Again

Cal Perkins and Mia Finley- Angels Above

Amore Island

Family Bonds- Hunter and Kayla

Family Bonds- Drew and Amanda

Family Bonds – Mac and Sidney

Family Bonds- Emily & Crew

Family Bonds- Ava & Seth

Family Bonds- Eli & Bella

Family Bonds- Hailey & Rex

Family Bonds- Penelope & Griffin

Family Bonds- Bode & Samantha

Family Bonds- Hudson & Delaney

Family Bonds- Alex & Jennie

Family Bonds- Roark & Chelsea

Family Bonds- Duke & Hadley

Family Bonds – Carter & Avery

Family Bonds- Egan & Blake

Family Bonds- Carson & Laine

Family Bonds- Grace & Lincoln

Blossoms

A Love for Lily – Zane Wolfe and Lily Bloom

A Playboy For Poppy- Reese McGill and Poppy Bloom

A Romantic For Rose – Thomas Klein and Rose Bloom

A Return For Ren – Ren Whitney and Zara Wolfe

A Journey For Jasmine- Wesley Wright and Jasmine Greene

A Vacationer for Violet – Violet Soren And Trace Mancini

A Hero For Heather- Heather Davis and Luke Remington

A Doctor For Daisy- Daisy Jones And Theo James

An Investigator For Ivy- Ivy Greene and Brooks Scarsdale

A Date For Dahlia- Dahlia Greene and Hugh Crosby

A Surprise For Sage- Sage Mancini and Knox Bradford

Looking For Love

Learning To Love – West Carlisle and Abby Sherman

Love To The Rescue – Braylon Carlisle and Lilian Baker

Love Collection

Vin Steele and Piper Fielding – Secret Love

Jared Hawk and Shelby McDonald – True Love

Erik McMann and Sheldon Case – Finding Love

Connor Landers and Melissa Mahoney- Beach Love

Ian Price and Cam Mason- Intense Love

Liam Sullivan and Ali Rogers - Autumn Love

Owen Taylor and Jill Duncan - Holiday Love

Chase Martin and Noelle Bennett - Christmas Love

Zeke Collins and Kendall Hendricks - Winter Love

Troy Walker and Meena Dawson – Chasing Love

Jace Stratton and Lauren Towne - First Love

Gabe Richards and Leah Morrison - Forever Love

Blake Wilson and Gemma Anderson – Simply Love

Brendan St. Nicholas and Holly Lane – Gifts of Love

ABOUT THE AUTHOR

Sign up for my newsletter for up to date releases and deals. Newsletter.

Follow me on:

Website
   Twitter
   Facebook
   Pinterest
   Goodreads
   Bookbub

As always reviews are always appreciated as they help potential readers understand what a book is about and boost rankings for search results.

Printed in Dunstable, United Kingdom